Achoo! Wait! Don't move . . . *Achoo!* Whew, that was close! I've got a witch-flu called *spellfluenza,* so when I sneeze, my powers jump into somebody else. Until I sneeze again, that is. But I *desperately* had to go to school today. It was a Harvey thing. And now I'm sneezing my powers all over the school! It's only a matter of time until they fly into the person who could make the *worst* use of them—Libby Chessler.

Libby, the Teenage Witch. I don't like the sound of that.

My name's Sabrina, and I'm sixteen. I always knew I was different, but I thought it was just because I lived with my strange aunts, Zelda and Hilda, while my divorced parents bounced around the world. Dad's in the foreign service. The *very* foreign service. He's a witch—and so am I.

I can't run to Mom—but *not* because she's currently on an archaeological dig in Peru. She's a mortal. If I set eyes on her in the next two years, she'll turn into a ball of wax. So for now, I'm stuck with my aunts. They're hanging around to show me everything I need to know about this witch business. They say all I have to do is concentrate and point. And I thought fitting in was tough!

You probably think I have superpowers. Think again! I can't turn back time and I'm on my own when it comes to love. Of course, there are some pretty neat things I *can* do—but that's where the trouble *always* begins. . . .

Sabrina, the Teenage Witch™ books

#1 Sabrina, the Teenage Witch
#2 Showdown at the Mall
#3 Good Switch, Bad Switch

Available from ARCHWAY Paperbacks

Good Switch, Bad Switch

David Cody Weiss and Bobbi JG Weiss

AN ARCHWAY PAPERBACK
Published by POCKET BOOKS
New York   London   Toronto   Sydney   Tokyo   Singapore

This book is a work of fiction. Names, characters, places and incidents are products of the author's imagination or are used fictitiously. Any resemblance to actual events or locales or persons, living or dead, is entirely coincidental.

AN ARCHWAY PAPERBACK *Original*

An Archway Paperback published by
POCKET BOOKS, a division of Simon & Schuster Inc.
1230 Avenue of the Americas, New York, NY 10020

ISBN: 0-671-01435-8

First Archway Paperback printing August 1997

10 9 8 7 6 5 4 3 2 1

AN ARCHWAY PAPERBACK and colophon are registered trademarks of Simon & Schuster Inc.

SABRINA THE TEENAGE WITCH and all related titles, logos and characters are trademarks of Archie Comics Publications, Inc.

Cover photo by Don Cadette

Printed in the U.S.A.

IL: 5+

To Robert and Kari—
   You guys got us into this mess in the first place.
                                      Thanks!

Good Switch, Bad Switch

Prologue

☆

The door to the linen closet burst open, spraying the darkened hallway with whorls of colored confetti. The cloud of paper cheer blew spirals around the two women who strode out of the closet laughing and chattering.

Unnoticed by Zelda and Hilda Spellman, a gauzy stream of golden sparkles wound in and around the confetti. Alive and yet not aware of being alive, the golden sparkles had intent without having a self to intend anything. As they moved, they sampled everything in their path, rejecting anything that did not match what they were seeking.

Golden sparkles brushed along Hilda's wrist as she covered a laugh. "Did you see that werewolf with the bald spot?" she cackled to her sister.

"I felt so embarrassed for him," said Zelda. "Why didn't anyone tell him?"

"With those teeth?" said Hilda, rubbing her nose. "It takes years to grow back a nose after it's been bitten off."

The hand that rubbed the nose had a flavor that attracted the sparkles. The flavor savored of power and witchery. The sparkles could live and breed only in a body that tasted like this. But there was something wrong. Something about the body was repelling the sparkles. They swarmed close to the skin, pushing until they came up against the faint residue of other, long-past golden sparkles.

The floating cloud drew back. The sparkles realized, without having anything that could analyze, reason, or respond, that the body that attracted them had already been colonized by their kind. The cloud undulated toward the other body.

"Anyway, that werewolf made a keynote speech that no one will ever forget, even if they can't remember what he said," chuckled Zelda. "By the way, why didn't Drell make the keynote speech for the biggest magical trade show of the year?"

The sparkles brushed against Zelda's hand and slipped onward, unrewarded. This body, too, had been colonized, and a long time ago at that. The sparkles sank down to the carpet. Perhaps they'd have to lie here for a century or two, until others of witch blood passed by to awaken them, as the two Spellman sisters had moments ago.

"Drell said,"—Zelda stiffened and affected a pompous air, obviously imitating the head of the Witches' Council— "'I've been the opening speaker of the Witches' Hexpo for so many years—it's time someone else had a chance.'"

"The promoters didn't ask him back this year, did they?"

"Nope."

Before the golden sparkles hit the carpet, they were caught by a draft that blew them under the door, into Sabrina's room. Slightly diffused by the breeze, the edges of the stream brushed against one of the girl's shoes and ribboned toward the cracks in the window casement. There was a creature sleeping below the window that momentarily attracted the sparkles. There was something about this furry black thing that hinted of witch-power, but it was a faint echo, as if power had dwelt there at one time, but was now absent.

Beyond the bedroom door, the aunts' voices softened as they headed down the hall toward their own rooms. "Well, at least Drell is taking it with grace," Zelda remarked.

"Nuh-uh," smirked her sister. "Didja see those two ugly little newts running around the Familiars and Accessories booth?"

"The ones that the asps from Serpent Supply kept trying to eat?"

"Yup. Those were the Hexpo promoters."

The draft through Sabrina's bedroom made the sleeping girl chilly. She rolled completely around as she floated above her bed, wrapping the covers around her like a mummy. The disturbance in the air was enough to stir up the tail end of the golden sparkles so that one touched her skin. A shiver ran through the cloud. This body had the right flavor. It also had no residue of previous colonization.

With a snap and a ripple, the entire cloud descended on the sleeping teenager, settling in to feed and reproduce.

Outside, Zelda stopped in front of her bedroom door, shaking her head at Hilda's revelation. "I hope they make it through the show. Drell can be so petty."

"You haven't heard the end of it. Drell sent the werewolf a cauldron of hair soup." With a wave, Hilda disappeared into her own bedroom.

In the bedroom opposite the linen closet, Sabrina began to sniffle.

Chapter 1

☆

☆

Sabrina's bedroom by morning light was no little girl's idyllic resting place. It was a fashion battlefield. Clothes were strewn across the bed and the floor. GUESS? sprawled atop Esprit under crumpled Danskins and crushed Betsey Johnsons. As a sort of tacky garnish, wads of tissue were scattered among the clothes. Along the bed sat three purses in a row: a sleek black leather clutch purse, a white leather satchel with teal and silver accents, and a Hello Kitty backpack.

Sabrina was frantic. "What do I wear, Salem?" she moaned to the black Burmese cat bathing on the window seat. "Today is like absolutely crucial to my entire future!" She stared at her reflection in the pewter-framed pier mirror. In quick succession she magicked on and off several outfits: a *Savvy* model creation in clashing colors,

5

a sleek *Vogue* pantsuit, a very Melrose study in black and black, and a very retro *Annie Hall*. "What would you wear?" she demanded.

"Sorry," Salem drawled. "My preferences wouldn't do you any good. It's not P.C. for humans to wear fur." His tongue rasped over a particularly unpleasant spot on his leg. "Though I wouldn't mind being able to send mine out to a cleaner's. Pfui!"

Sabrina kicked a sock at the cat, who started to bat at it, but remembered his dignity and turned the movement into a slow, deliberate stretch. "What's so big about today? I thought you weren't going out with Harvey until the weekend."

"This is not about Harvey, as if that were any of your business. This is about my chance to broaden my horizons, to participate in a world beyond this small, provincial town." Her hands rose slowly, spreading out as if they were the petals of a flower. The effect was strangely magnified by the two balls of uncrumpling tissue expanding in her hands. "To become an instrument and play for the masses the pathos of life and the tragedies of the soul."

Salem yawned. "If you win an Oscar, I promise not to knock it off the mantel."

Sabrina yanked a cranberry pullover out from under the cat, sending him rolling backward. "You're just jealous because you can't become a famous actor."

Salem lay on his back, all four legs splayed. "I don't have to. Cats have humans imitating them on Broadway, and other humans pay to see them do it. Face it, cats domesticated people. Mortals, anyway."

"Like you can take credit for it. You're only temporarily a cat." Salem had been a witch who had gotten caught trying to take over the world. The Witches' Council had stripped him of his powers and condemned him to spend a hundred years as an ordinary house cat. Well, maybe not so ordinary. He could carry on quite an intelligent conversation when he wanted to. Or he could be a brat.

"Convict me on a technicality, why don't you?" said Salem. "Anyway, it's just an audition for a drama club."

Sabrina dabbed at her nose with a tissue before she corrected Salem. "It's a Thespian Society," she said. When Salem rolled his eyes at her, she pouted her lip defensively. "Well, that's what they call it here." A smile cracked her face. It grew into a grin. "Okay, it's stupid. But what do you expect from a high school whose football team is called the Fighting Scallions?"

"I'd expect a—"

Salem's retort was cut off when Sabrina sneezed explosively. She ripped tissues out of a box and jammed them to her nose, but she didn't sneeze again. Hesitantly, she lowered the tissues.

Nothing happened.

A stray realization hit Sabrina. She turned to Salem. "You didn't say anything!"

Salem arched his head back and stared up at her over his nose. "Ex-cuse me?"

"When I sneezed," Sabrina explained. "You didn't say anything. Normally people say 'gesundheit' or 'bless you' or something like that when a person sneezes. Why didn't you say anything?"

"Listen, the only reason humans say those sort of things is because their ancestors believed that their essence could escape when they sneezed. I'm a cat. The only thing that escapes when I sneeze is loose hair. No comments are needed."

"Oh, we're back to the 'cat' defense again, eh? That's going to wear thin one day, Salem. You're going to be a witch again someday, with all your powers back. You need to seriously think about how you're going to handle that."

"Sure. I'll arrange for a wake-up call to remind me just before it happens. You know of a service that books decades ahead?" He looked over at the clock radio on Sabrina's nightstand. "And speaking of reminders . . . you're late!"

"Eeek! I still have to shower!" Sabrina snatched up her bathrobe and blew out the door to the bathroom. Behind her, she heard Salem mutter, "Of course, if I could magic up whatever I wanted again . . ." Then she was in the bathroom, yanking on the old-style taps in the shower stall. She turned the water up hot.

A moment later, Sabrina was under the shower, letting the hot, stinging drops bring circulation to her skin. She soaked up the warmth and relaxed with a contented sigh. New England was a nice place, but it seemed too cold for half the year. Sabrina hadn't gotten used to it yet.

Growing up with her parents hadn't been a textbook case in stability. Between her mother's penchant for digging up ancient thingies in impossibly remote parts of the world and her father's mysterious work in the Foreign Service that moved him around as well, Sabrina hadn't spent much time in any one place for . . . well, years.

For reasons that Sabrina skirted thinking about, her parents had divorced when she was only ten years old. Already burdened with the isolation of being an only child, the relocations and the family breakup made a rich interior fantasy life a necessity. Sometimes those fantasies became a bit too persistent, such as her irrational hope that somehow her parents would get back together again. Sabrina dreamed that dramatic training would give her a handle on all the conflicting feelings that constantly surged within her. The Thespian Society also offered the hope of belonging to some social group in a new school and town where she was automatically an outsider. And, if nothing else, it might give her chances to practice love scenes with Harvey.

Westbridge was small and quiet, maybe even a little dull, but that was okay by Sabrina. Her agenda was booked solid. First and foremost, every day she woke up four feet above her bed— a clear reminder that since her sixteenth birthday she'd become a witch, with real supernatural powers.

Second, she'd trot down the stairs to greet Aunt Hilda and Aunt Zelda, both reinforcements of the witch thing, since they were both witches. They were also reminders of her parents' divorce. Since Edward Spellman and his wife had split up, there was this little problem about Sabrina's mom turning into a ball of wax if she set eyes on her daughter in the next two years. Her two aunts were all Sabrina had by way of family for a while. There was another aunt named Vesta whom she had met, but the older witch lived in another realm called the Pleasure Zone and pursued a high-octane life of hedonism that Sabrina didn't think would fit into anybody's definition of family values.

The third and fourth items on her schedule kicked in at Westbridge High School. Life as a transfer student doesn't have to be a living hell. People don't have to go out of their way to ridicule you, sneer at you, and make you the butt of jokes. People don't have to, but Libby Chessler did. With a spoon.

But then, as if to make up for Libby—in fact, as if to make up for everything and leave a warm, satisfying surplus—there was Harvey. Harvey Dwight Kinkle. Shy hunk, solo dancer, secret thinker, and, at last check, Sabrina's soul mate.

Who was also going to be at this afternoon's audition, right after school, which Sabrina was nearly late for.

Sabrina reluctantly left the warm embrace of the shower, toweled off, and slipped back into her robe. She was drying her hair when she noticed that, although her nose was still a little stuffy, she hadn't sneezed again. *Great! Like I need a cold before an audition,* she thought. *Ladies and gentlemen—Miss Scarlett O'Hara. "Tomorrow is another ACHEW!"*

Sabrina looked at her face in the mirror. It seemed healthy enough. She peered closely at her eyes. Golden sparkles danced for an instant in her pupils, but a blink later they were gone. *Might as well start fighting it now,* Sabrina thought, reaching for the chewable vitamin C's.

She popped three orange-flavored wafers and was crunching them noisily as she opened the bathroom door and padded barefoot down the hall, avoiding the cold hardwood floors by keeping to the Persian carpet runners. As she approached her bedroom, her nose suddenly wrinkled at the unmistakable smell of the ocean at low tide. There was a strange slapping sort of noise coming from her bedroom. Sabrina yanked the door open and froze in stunned surprise.

Her room was filled ankle-deep with fish! Carp, sturgeon, bream, tuna, bonito, trout, flounder, catfish, bass, cod—kinds Sabrina couldn't even recognize. Alive. All of them. Flopping and wriggling around the floor, under her bed, on her clothes!

And sitting on her bed in the center of it all, a fish hanging out of his mouth and eyes bugging out like a deer caught in headlights, was Salem.

Chapter 2

Sabrina stood, shocked, in the doorway long enough for Salem to drop the fish. "What is going on here?" she shrieked.

Salem took a moment to lick off a smear of glittering scales that streaked one paw. Looking out the window, he said, "My guess is that someone took pity on me and fulfilled my heart's desire."

Sabrina threw up her hands in frustration. "I mean, where did all these fish come from?"

"What I said."

"Never mind. I'm late for school so your heaven is going to have to wait." Sabrina waved her arms at the room. "Fish, be gone!" she commanded.

Nothing happened. The fish continued to flop

around, and a large eel wriggled through the cranberry pullover on the bed.

"The fish are still here. What did I do wrong?" Sabrina felt a cold sting in the pit of her stomach. Since gaining her powers, she had complained many times of how they had complicated her life. But she had never really given any thought to how she would feel if they suddenly ceased to work.

"Why are you asking me?" said Salem. "It's not as if I could twitch my tail and wish for unlimited milk to go along with all these fish." He did twitch his tail, though, and an instant later a cow was standing between Sabrina's bed and the desk. It looked at the fish with some nervousness and gave a loud "Mooooo." Then it lipped up some papers from the desk and started chewing.

"That's my homework!" shrieked Sabrina. She jabbed her finger at the cow and the fish. "Be gone! Be gone! Be gone!"

The fish continued to flop around on the floor. The cow looked at Sabrina with vague cow contentment and continued chewing.

With a desperate "Aaagh!" Sabrina fled the room, thundering down the stairs to the kitchen. "Aunt Zelda! Aunt Hilda! Help!"

The ground floor was silent. There was a large note written on lavender-scented paper propped up on the toaster. As Sabrina snatched it up, Zelda's voice floated up from the paper.

"Good morning, Sabrina," the note said cheerfully. "Hilda and I had so much fun at the Witches' Hexpo yesterday that we're getting an early start today. Don't wait supper for us, just conjure up something for yourself. Love you."

Sabrina gaped in confusion. For a moment her brain vapor-locked, not processing anything but pure dismay. Then her nose started running again. She snatched a paper towel and pressed it to her face. "This isn't happening," she growled. "This is *not* happening!"

She ran back upstairs to her room. To her surprise, the fish-strewn floor now swarmed with cats as well. They gnawed at fish or wound themselves around the cow's legs, gazing longingly up at her udder.

"Come on in and join the celebration," Salem called out jovially. "I don't know how it happened, but I've got my witch powers back! I invited some friends in to celebrate. Hey, do you want me to magic you up some breakfast? Lox and eggs? Kippers? Sugar-frosted fish flakes?"

A tickle formed behind Sabrina's nose, just in front of the throbbing sensation that filled her head almost to bursting. "Those are *my* ah . . . mmph," she stifled a sneeze, ". . . powers!" The tickle grew in intensity. It was maddening. As Sabrina struggled against the building sneeze she grew furious. "I don't know . . . aahh . . . how they got away, but I want them . . . ahhh . . . back and I . . . ahh . . . ahh . . . CHOO!" The sneeze burst from her lips with unexpected violence, and a tingling shiver ran through her body as an aftershock. Automatically, she finished her sentence. ". . . want all this stuff gone!"

The silence that followed was stunning. The cats were gone. The fish were gone. The cow was gone. And so, unfortunately, was Sabrina's homework.

Sabrina stared at her room in confusion. "What just happened?"

Salem sniffed dismissively and strolled back to his place in the bay window. "Since all my goodies are gone, my guess is that you've got your powers back and I'm a slave to the can opener again." He kept his back to Sabrina and stared moodily out the stained glass panels.

"Duh, Sherlock," said Sabrina. "I guessed that much. I mean, why did that happen?"

"Ask your aunts. I'm just a powerless cat, remember?"

"I can't. They're away at that trade show."

"Then try the book."

When Sabrina turned sixteen and her aunts had told her that she was a witch, they had also given her a present from her father—a book entitled *The Discovery of Magic*. The book, which was enormous and stood on a lectern of its own in Sabrina's bedroom, contained all the spells and conjurings that Sabrina was supposed to learn in order to be a proper practicing witch.

Sabrina opened the heavy cover and flipped to the index. "Witches, diseases of . . ." she read. "See Witch Doctor." She glared over at the cat, who was still intently staring at anything else in the room other than Sabrina. "Oh, fine. I have a problem and the book hands me old jokes."

"What joke?" drawled Salem. "Who else would witches see when they're sick?"

Sabrina's finger ran down the long columns of tiny print. " 'Witch Doctor . . . page 273.' There really *is* such a thing." Sabrina marveled as she riffled forward.

A voice that would have put James Earl Jones to shame boomed up from the book. "It is very impolite to doubt someone's existence. Where would you be if I chose to disbelieve in you, young lady?"

"Uh . . . right here?" Sabrina guessed. The voice had come from a richly detailed illustration of a dark man in dreadlocks whose skin bore intricate tattoos. Delicately carved ivory skewers pierced his nose, ears, and eyebrows. Gaudy feathers, fetishes, and mojo bags were tied around his neck and wrists. He was, in fact, the very picture of a classic witch doctor except for the pencil-stripe Armani suit and the cell phone in his hand.

"Not likely," the illustration laughed. His amusement puzzled Sabrina but seemed to erase the witch doctor's initial grumpiness. "To business! What are your symptoms?"

"Well, I have a runny nose, I sneeze, and—oh, yes—my powers disappeared."

"Hmmm. I see. Turn the page and cough."

Sabrina paused. "What?"

"I need a sample to analyze," the witch doctor explained impatiently. "Turn the page and cough into it."

With a shrug to Salem, Sabrina did as she was instructed. Then she turned back the page to look at the witch doctor again. He was shaking a jewel-encrusted silver rattle over a small glass microscope slide. A cloud of golden sparkles rose from the slide as if sucked up by the rattle. The sparkles disappeared into it, and a moment later a piece of paper shot out of the handle.

The witch doctor beamed at the rattle as he grabbed the diagnosis in midair. "Fabergé makes the best medical tools," he remarked before turning his attention to the paper. His smile faded and he shook his head. "Oh, this is bad. Very bad."

"What is it?" asked Sabrina in alarm.

"It's a memo from my broker telling me that my stocks are losing money." He gave Sabrina a sheepish grin as he shook the rattle. "I left it on 'fax' accidentally." He pressed some beads on the handle and another slip of paper shot out. "You have a case of spellfluenza," he finally announced, his eyes skimming the readout. "It lasts twenty-four hours. Avoid all contact with nonwitches until it goes away." Giving Sabrina a reassuring nod, he concluded, "Good day!" and started reaching for his cell phone.

"Wait a minute!" Sabrina said quickly. "You have to tell me more than *that.*"

"No, I don't. Rule number one of the medical profession: Time is money. I have to call my broker."

"I'll report you to the Witches' Council!"

The doctor's face split with a brilliant white smile. For the first time, Sabrina noticed that his teeth were filed to points. "Oh, please do," he hissed. "Drell still owes me for curing his case of nose mites. I won't do anything for him until he pays—anything *good,* that is."

"Cut her some slack, doc," broke in Salem. "She's just turned sixteen. This is all new to her."

The doctor produced a pair of pince-nez spectacles out of nowhere and peered up at Sabrina through them. "Ah, you're really as young as you seem, then. Sorry, I thought you were an old biddy with an overambitious youth spell." The spectacles vanished.

"You have an acute case of spellfluenza. This is what we call a witch-specific malady; that is, it only attacks persons with witch-power. Its symptoms are similar to that of an ordinary cold—sniffles, postnasal drip, headache, loss of appetite, et cetera, et cetera—with the exception that if you sneeze, your witch-powers fly out of you.

"If you are alone in a room, the powers will bounce back to you automatically. But if there are mortals present, the powers will settle into one of them. And that is where they will stay, until you sneeze a second time in that person's presence. Then your powers will return. This is why I recommend that you avoid all mortal contact for the next twenty-four hours."

"But I can't stay home," Sabrina declared. "I have to go to school today."

"If you sneeze, you could lose your powers to someone else," the witch doctor warned her, wagging his finger.

"Oh, what's the big deal?" asked Salem. "All she has to do is to sneeze again. Or carry pepper with her."

"Sorry. Fake sneezes won't do the trick. They have to be genuine. And I don't even want to think about the trouble pepper could cause." He tapped at some beads on the handle of the rattle and stared at the paper it spat out. "Multiple sneezes in rapid succession would have her powers ricocheting through the room. It could get ugly."

"So how do I keep myself from sneezing at school?" Sabrina asked.

"I don't know. Maybe vitamin C?"

Sabrina glared at the witch doctor.

He shook his rattle limply at her. "There's only so much that modern medicine can do."

Chapter 3

Sabrina crunched another orange-flavored wafer as she slumped through the door of biology class. She had made it this far into the school day without sneezing, but the tension she was under had her walking around hunched over and curled in on herself. She was moving so slowly that the other students pushed past her to get into the classroom. "Excuse me," she grumbled when somebody jostled her elbow.

Sabrina found her stool, dropped her bookbag, and slowly eased herself down. The witch doctor hadn't said anything about spellfluenza symptoms including aching joints that creaked audibly as she moved. She leaned forward, propping her head up on her hands, wishing she could just melt to the floor and take a nice, long, comfortable nap.

"Gee, I wish I had your concentration!" Jenny was suddenly at Sabrina's side, settling into her place.

"Huh?" Sabrina grunted.

"You must have chosen a really heavy piece to do," Jenny beamed. She took another look at her friend, as if reassessing her. "You know, I never would have taken you for a Method actor."

"What are you talking about, Jenny? I'm not acting, I'm sick," Sabrina moaned.

"Aren't there laws against people coming to school with communicable diseases?" a new voice broke in. "Something in the Sanitation Code?"

Sabrina lifted her head to glare at the captain of the cheerleaders, who was sauntering into the classroom. "I'm not infectious, Libby. At least not here." With all that was on her mind, the last thing Sabrina wanted was to have a run-in with Libby.

Libby apparently had nothing better to do at the moment than get under Sabrina's skin. "I mean it," she complained, dropping her books loudly on her lab table. "It should be illegal for me to have to sit near a diseased freak."

Sabrina felt her patience fraying. It was at times like these that having witch-powers available for paybacks was a wicked temptation. But there was satisfaction to be had in subtlety as well. Leaning over toward her tormentor, Sabrina said, "I told you, Libby, I'm not—hey, what's that weird spot on your neck?"

Libby's eyes grew wide and she clapped a hand to her throat. "What? Where?" She tried to look down far enough to see the spot, which was, of course, physically impossible. Sabrina stifled a grin and heard Jenny snort with amusement as Libby jumped to her feet. "I have to go find a mirror!" Leaving one hand covering her throat, Libby snatched up her purse with the other and ran out of the classroom.

Jenny clapped her hands together, bursting with glee. "You are *so* mean!" she bubbled to Sabrina.

"Not that Libby doesn't deserve it." Sabrina smiled tiredly and lowered her head to the lab table.

Jenny shifted her weight slightly on her stool. "You were serious about the not-infectious part, weren't you?"

"Huh?" Sabrina lifted her head. "Oh, yeah. It's just a sniffle I picked up at home. It's sort of a family-specific cold." She dabbed at her reddened nose with a tissue.

Jenny made a show of pulling her stool up to the table, in her usual place right next to Sabrina. "Well, if you're sure. I don't want anything to spoil my audition this afternoon."

Sabrina bolted upright. "Ohmigosh, I forgot about the audition! I still haven't chosen what to read!"

"Oh, Sabrina!" laughed Jenny. "I'm sure they've got speeches they could hand you. You'd have to do a cold reading, though," she added seriously.

Sabrina had just pulled a fresh tissue out of a pack. She stopped and stared at Jenny. Jenny suddenly caught the accidental joke and burst out laughing. Sabrina collapsed in laughter as well.

The class bell rang and the milling students hustled to their places at the six Formica-topped lab tables. As they focused their attention on the front of the room, they noticed that Mr. Pool's desk had been moved to the far corner of the room and in its place stood a low, wide table. Atop the table, like a 3-D model of an ingrown plumbing system, sprawled a conglomeration of hamster habitat tubes. There were several dead ends to the tube complex, some of which had baskets of treats, while others ended on shiny electrode disks.

Mr. Pool shuffled into the room, carrying a cage filled with six white mice. "For tomorrow's unit on behaviorism and electric shock reinforcement," he said, setting the mice down next to the habitat. Hearing Jenny and Sabrina still laughing, he cast a vinegary smile at the two girls. "I'm overjoyed to see you so glad to be here, ladies. Perhaps you could cheer me up by being the first to turn in your homework assignments."

The pit of Sabrina's stomach sank. "Uh, Mr. Pool . . ." she began.

Pool sauntered over to her table, his face set in its customary expression of world-weary annoyance. "Is this the part where you concoct some highly unlikely but desperately plausible excuse for not having your homework, Miss Spellman?" He placed his hands like fans behind his ears. "Go ahead, I'm all ears."

"M-my homework was . . ." Sabrina's voice dropped to a barely audible whisper. ". . . eaten by a cow."

"Eaten by a cow." Mr. Pool rubbed his hands together as if checking the texture of Sabrina's excuse between his palms. "First time I've ever been told that. You get an *F* for the day, but an *A* for originality." He turned around and started heading back to the front of the class just as Libby burst through the door.

Glaring in Sabrina's direction, Libby stalked to her chair and sat down. Her face looked like it had been roughly scrubbed and the makeup hastily reapplied. Mr. Pool whirled on her. "I believe you're supposed to arrive *before* the bell rings, Miss Chessler." He glanced up at the ceiling. "Unless you want to tell me that you were delayed by a rampaging bovine ruminant."

The entire class burst into laughter, and Libby flushed from her toes to her scalp. She didn't know why everyone was laughing at her, but she was sure that Sabrina Spellman was at the bottom of it. She threw Sabrina a withering glare, but Sabrina ducked the cheerleader's wrath by concentrating on finding the current chapter in her textbook. Libby grudgingly turned back around, Mr. Pool began droning on about osmosis and hypertonic solutions, and the world reduced itself to a gently throbbing ache inside Sabrina's head.

The itch in her nostrils awoke without warning. Sabrina jerked upright with a small gasp and grabbed for her tissues.

Mr. Pool, who had just stabbed a potato with an electrode, blinked out at her. "No need to get upset, Miss Spellman. The potato didn't feel a thing."

Sabrina didn't answer—the itch was a dagger of fire between her watery eyes, and all her attention had gathered right at that spot, anticipating a sneeze of epic proportions.

Mr. Pool pierced the potato with a second electrode, then gathered both electrodes' wires and jacked them into a small black box with a 75-watt light bulb screwed into a fixture at the top. "This humble little potato will now demonstrate the electroconductive properties of living things—the galvanic principle—named after the brilliant Italian physiologist, Luigi Galvani."

Sabrina tried tightly pinching her nose, hoping that external pain would stop or distract the internal itch. She didn't hear Mr. Pool mutter, as the bulb remained dark, "Oh, drat it all! This stupid demonstration never works for me!" And because the sneeze that erupted at that moment nearly deafened her, Sabrina didn't hear the science teacher swear under his breath, or see him point an accusing finger at the errant experiment. "I wish for once that this thing would *work!*"

Sabrina's ears may have been ringing, but there was nothing wrong with her eyes. She, and the rest of the class, saw the bulb on top of the black box suddenly light up. They also saw the potato start quivering, smoke rising from the electrodes and sending the aroma of baked potato through the room. But only Sabrina knew why it was happening. Her witch-powers must have zapped into Mr. Pool when she sneezed, and he had magicked the experiment into working! Supernatural energy was powering that light, making it shine brighter and brighter by the instant. Sabrina suddenly knew what was next. "Get down!" she shouted.

Everyone was so unnerved by the strange experiment that they were primed. At Sabrina's shout they dived for the deck, even Mr. Pool. So when the light bulb exploded a moment later, no one was hit by flying glass.

Jenny yelped in surprise and threw herself at Sabrina as they huddled under their stools. Jenny's long, tightly curled red hair billowed around Sabrina's face, reawakening the sinus itch. Sabrina immediately sneezed again.

This time, Sabrina could feel her powers return, like a favorite old flannel shirt, soft enough to disappear from sensation moments after it's put on. She breathed a sigh of relief as the class bell rang. This power-switching business could be dangerous!

Lunch should have been a time for Sabrina to relax and marshal her strength, but the spellfluenza made that impossible. The vitamin C tablets made her tongue feel like a toxic-waste dump. And the cafeteria food, never better than passable on good days, made Sabrina's belly do the Macarena at the very sight of it. Maybe staying home would have been better than dealing with a case of spellfluenza at school after all.

Sabrina also found herself compulsively counting the number of people in whatever room she was in when her nose started to itch. So many bodies for her powers to leap into if she sneezed. And how could she tell who got them, unless that person did something extraordinary while Sabrina was there to see?

She wanted to sit alone, but Westbridge High had a small cafeteria, and each clique laid claim to territory and defended it ferally.

Libby ruled over the official Cool Table, surrounded by her lackeys and the boys they were teasing that week. Hisses, punctuated by giggles, rose from the customary cloud of perfume and cosmetics. Sabrina's welcome there would make absolute zero feel warm.

The jocks sat in the furthest corner of the room, as if they could hide from notice there like they did in the backs of classrooms. Their table was rowdy, with oversized humor and random bits of flying food. Sabrina could sit there, but she'd have to smile and giggle mindlessly to do it.

The nerd table was sweatily male, and its denizens spoke a language no one else could translate. There were always free spaces at their table, but girls avoided it, as if nerdism was a communicable disease. Besides, girls made the nerds twitch with nervousness.

Nobody sat with the freshmen.

That left the no-man's-land table in the middle. Only the misfits and the uncommitted sat there, branded as outsiders by their choice of table companions. This was where Sabrina, Jenny, and Harvey always sat. Since neither of them had arrived yet, Sabrina reluctantly took her usual place. Maybe, if she was lucky, her friends wouldn't show.

Luck wasn't with her. Jenny waltzed past on her way to the food line. She had a playbook open in her hands and was reading lines silently to herself. As if to demonstrate that luck wasn't even thinking about Sabrina Spellman at that moment, Sabrina sneezed several times in rapid succession.

She could feel the ricochet of her powers fleeing and returning, like tiny outward and inward tuggings at her body. She gasped in shock at the repeated sensation; then the sneezing stopped, and her nose settled down to a slow drip again.

A horrible thought struck her. *Did I sneeze an even number of times or an odd number of times? Do I still have my powers?*

She pointed her finger at her milk, willing it to become chocolate milk instead. Nothing happened. Sabrina's finger wilted, and she scanned the cafeteria quickly. There were so many people around! *Who's got my powers?* she thought in panic. *Libby? Jill? Cee Cee? Gordie? Sasha? Quick—somebody do something magical!*

Jenny came breezing over from the cashier's, balancing her tray in one hand and the playbook in the other. She was navigating her way across the room without taking her eyes from the book, her lips moving as she recited lines to herself. When she got to the table, she hooked a chair out with one foot and lowered herself, her tray, and her book all in one smooth motion.

Then she flew back up like a red-haired rocket, swatting at the back of her pants and shouting angrily, "Eww! Gross! Who left this mess on the chair?"

"It's only a crumpled napkin," said Sabrina. "A dry one. You didn't get stained."

"That's not the point," said Jenny angrily as she dragged the chair away from the table and replaced it with a different one. "Leaving trash around is a sign of incivility and social discourtesy. If we can't get along well enough to agree not to litter, what hope is there for solving any of the greater problems of the world?" She held up the offending napkin, gripped between her fingernails. "This may be only a napkin to you, but it's the death knell of humanity to me."

Jenny held the napkin out at arm's length and marched over to the trash. As usual, the trash slot in the wall was a mess, with paper cups and gloppy trays poking out, dirty napkins dangling, and a congregation of crumbs on the floor beneath. Students had jammed their trays and leftovers in so awkwardly that the slot was blocked, and no trays or plates could make it to the conveyor belt to the dishwasher. The whole thing looked like a booby trap.

Jenny leaned over, trying to find a place to deposit her napkin without triggering a trash avalanche. There was a slice of half-eaten pizza that looked oily enough. She carefully leaned the napkin against the slice until the oils latched on to the paper. In seconds, the napkin was bonded to the pizza slice and in no danger of sliding off.

Jenny leaped back and shook her hands in disgust. "There was no reason that I had to do that," she complained. "I wish somebody besides me cared about trash!"

"Is something wrong, Miss Kelly?" boomed a voice directly behind Jenny.

"P-p-principal LaRue," stammered Jenny. "I'm sorry. I didn't mean to make such a fuss."

The nattily dressed head of Westbridge High School towered over the slim girl, his tidy bulk as threatening as an avalanche waiting to cut loose. "About trash?" LaRue acted surprised. "Nonsense, young lady. Tidiness and civility go hand in hand. Why, picking up trash is probably humanity's oldest act." He fished a massive key ring out of his pants pocket, coiling up its long chain as he went. The keys rang musically as he sorted through them, looking for a specific key. He singled out a battered brass number and used it to unlock the door next to the trash slot.

The principal's actions weren't going unnoticed. All eyes in the cafeteria became riveted on the big man's back as he shucked his suit jacket, opened the door, and hung the jacket on a hook on the door's inner side. He stepped inside, shutting the door behind him.

Now everyone in the room was openly staring, wondering what was going on. Suddenly, immaculately manicured hands dug into the jumble of trays and began pulling them apart. Silverware jingled and glasses clinked as the principal deftly sorted trays from trash, loading the conveyor to the dishwasher.

Sabrina gaped, as stunned as the rest of her peers. Had the old man suddenly gone whack? What could make him want to clean trash—with his own hands? Then she realized. *Because Jenny wanted him to. Jenny has my powers!* Sabrina's eyes raked the cafeteria, but the willowy redhead was nowhere to be seen.

Chapter 4

Sabrina's eyes flicked toward the clock on the wall. She had ten minutes to find Jenny before the bell rang, sending them off to different classes for the next period. While casting spells required concentration and, in most cases, a definite knowledge that magic was being used, a mortal could do a lot of unintentional damage. The magic worked by Mr. Pool and Jenny was a result of their intense desire, a casual hand gesture, and, luckily, positive mental attitudes. *I'd hate to imagine what a nasty person could do with my powers,* thought Sabrina.

She ran out the cafeteria doors and glanced up and down the hallway. With a mountain of smoldering flame for hair, Jenny would have been hard to miss in a crowded hall. Now, during class time, the halls were unfamiliarly empty and it was easy for Sabrina to see that her friend wasn't there. Jenny was steamed, Sabrina thought quickly. Where would she go to cool off?

Remembering Jenny's focus on her playbook, Sabrina sprinted for the library, but a look through the doorway proved she wasn't there either. Sabrina slumped against the door, feeling doomed.

Then a shiver ran through her body and stalled deep in her nose. An itch the size of New England rippled across her sinuses. *Rats!* thought Sabrina. *I get my powers stolen by a magic cold, but I still have the cold!* Tears welling up in her eyes, she stumbled toward the girls' room.

She pushed the door open and felt it bang into a body on the other side. "Sorry," she sniffled as she headed for the sink at top speed.

"Hey! Watch where you're going!" a familiar voice said.

"Jenny?" called Sabrina, and she whirled around, catching a glimpse of Jenny's back just before the door closed. The urge to sneeze swelled inside her, threatening to explode. "Jenny!" Sabrina dashed for the door. "Wait, don't leave!" She yanked the door open with all her might and threw herself after her friend.

Surprised by the tone in Sabrina's voice, Jenny whirled around in concern. "Sabrina, what is it? What's wrong?"

"Jenny, I have—" Sabrina never got to finish

her sentence. The sneeze that had been roiling around inside her burst like a geyser.

Jenny staggered back, horrified, her hands flailing about as she looked down at her outfit in disgust. "Aaghh! You sneezed on me! Oh, how gross! Oh, this is soooo gross!" She broke and ran back to the girls' room.

Too late, Sabrina wadded tissues against her nose. "Denny . . . I'm dorry!" she began, but it was too late. The door to the girls' room slammed shut in her face.

If this isn't the worst day of my life, I don't want to know what could beat it, Sabrina thought as she headed back to the cafeteria. Turning the corner, she was almost run over by a furious Principal LaRue. His fists were clenched and his normally immaculate suit was stained with a garnish of shredded lettuce. He seemed not to see Sabrina at all, and only a quick flattening against the brick wall saved her from being trampled.

Unnerved by this, Sabrina headed back to the table where Harvey still sat, his eyes closed and his lips moving as he silently ran through his lines.

"Is everybody taking collision pills today?" Sabrina demanded as she plumped down into the chair across from Harvey. "First I almost deck Jenny, then LaRue almost flattens me. What made him so cheesed off, anyway?"

Harvey opened his eyes and blinked in

thought. "Well, he was busing trays over in the slot, and—"

Sabrina feigned shock. "Principal LaRue? *Our* Principal LaRue? The one who's so afraid of getting dirty he has Mr. Pool dust his chair before he sits in it?"

"Yeah," Harvey affirmed, bobbing his head in agreement. "I thought it was kinda strange at the time,"

Sabrina leaned back in the chair and tried to put events in perspective. *Jenny's command made LaRue clean up trash in the first place. That means the effects of her magic disappeared when my powers came back to me.* Sabrina made a wry face. *That's one consolation.*

Jenny walked up to the table and pointedly sat as far away from Sabrina as she could. Sabrina tried smiling at her friend, but Jenny buried her head in her playbook. *Is the price of getting my powers back going to be losing my best friend?*

Sabrina turned back to Harvey. "So, you want to work on geometry together in study hall?"

"Uh . . . sorry," Harvey said with difficulty. "See, Mr. Pool is letting me skip study hall to go to the Angle to practice my reading." He flushed a little, looking terribly apologetic. Harvey had a problem with saying "no."

Sabrina forced cheerfulness into her voice. "Oh. Well, I guess I'll see you at the auditions then."

Harvey brightened. "Sure," he grinned. Harvey liked it when things turned out for the best in the end.

The bell rang and everyone shuffled out of the cafeteria and into the hall. The crowd leaving collided with the eager beavers of the fifth period lunch shift, who raced inside to get in the food line first. Between the bodies pushing their way in and the bodies pushing their way out, Sabrina felt like a moth in a blender. Dizziness swept over her, and her head suddenly began to throb. A familiar itch made her start. *Oh, no!* Sabrina screamed silently. *I can't sneeze now! I can't! I can't!*

She could. The sneeze ricocheted through her head and she felt the fading tingle of her powers leaving. The sneeze also cleared a space around her as her fellow students gave her a wide berth, muttering in annoyance and casting dirty looks at her as if she were Death itself.

Sabrina's head snapped back and forth, scanning the surging crowd around her. *Oh, no, where have my powers gone now?*

Harvey settled himself under the big oak tree that filled most of the angular corner of grassy ground between the main school building and the gym extension. This shady spot overlooked the entire town of Westbridge and made for a retreat that had become Harvey's favorite place to think. He dug a dog-eared paperback out of his bag and opened it to his bookmark, folding the cover back so he could hold the book in one hand to read.

The Angle was the only place at school where Harvey didn't feel pressured. Everyone always seemed to expect something of him and expected him to do something about it . . . whatever "it" was. Teachers, peers, advertisers, bus drivers, librarians, everybody always seemed to be waiting for him to fulfill some expectation of theirs. His father had the most expectations of all. Being a hard-core sports fan, he'd already bought a big oak-and-glass display case to hold Harvey's sports trophies. Unfortunately, Harvey wasn't all that sure that a life of sweat and cumulative injuries was what he wanted.

The fact was, Harvey didn't really know what he wanted to do with his life. Sports were fun, of course, but—for instance, during just this past year—he had discovered that reading was fun, too. And at times, he'd start thinking again about being a dentist.

He had always kept it a secret from his friends that he liked to just sit and think. Life was an endlessly fascinating puzzle to Harvey, and he found it helpful to just sit and ponder the things that people did, and why they did them, and why he himself did what he did. The few times he had casually mentioned this pastime, however, everyone had sort of looked at him funny.

Except Sabrina, of course. But then again, Sabrina was the only person he knew who didn't expect things from him. She laughed at his jokes and was a great Foosball player. There seemed to be a lot more going on with her than she let on, and that tempted Harvey to let her in on his own secret world. If only he didn't become so darned shy around her.

As usual, when he thought about Sabrina, Harvey's insides churned in a funny sort of way. He sighed. He'd be better off putting those unruly emotions to work in his audition reading. He wriggled his shoulders around, loosening the muscles, then took a deep breath and began reading aloud from his book. " 'Don't you understand? They're no different than we are! They feel, they care, they—*love.* There's no reason to hate anymore. There's no reason to fight anymore. If we all extend the hand of friendship' " —and Harvey extended his arm stiffly, as if to shake an invisible hand—" 'we can bridge the gulf between us. Come. Let us all gather together in peace.' "

A feeling of warmth flickered through him, as if the words he was reading suddenly had meaning beyond the echo they left in the air. Then, to his surprise, a bird landed upon his outstretched hand.

Everyone in study hall was staring at Sabrina from behind their books. It was no wonder, because Sabrina had been sneezing regularly since she had taken her seat. The only person who didn't notice her was Mr. Pool, nominally in charge of the study hall that day, but actually deeply buried in the Personal-Classifieds of *Popular Scientist* magazine.

Try as she might, Sabrina couldn't concentrate on the open textbook before her. Visions of an unknown mortal running amok with her powers unreeled before her inner eye. The possibilities for disaster were awesome! Why, with witch-power, even common phrases could be dangerous. What if they pointed at someone and told them to "get lost"? What if they said "drop dead"? Sabrina began to sweat.

And what would happen to her when the Witches' Council heard about this? Her Aunt Hilda dated Drell, the head of the Council, but Sabrina didn't think that would help any. By his own admission, Drell was a vindictive, petty, spiteful, power-mad despot, and infuriatingly cheerful about it. He had sentenced Salem to be a cat for a hundred years. What would he do to Sabrina? A cold shiver ran through her body.

"If you're sick, why didn't you stay home?" hissed a voice behind her.

That caught Mr. Pool's attention. "Aren't you feeling well, Miss Spellman?" he asked over his magazine.

I feel rotten! Sabrina wanted to scream. *I've lost my powers and I'm sick to boot!* Instead, she smiled weakly at the teacher. "Just a twenty-four-hour bug. Nothing that anyone else could catch."

"Let's not let *you* be the judge of that, Missy. If you have something infectious, I could catch it and lose workdays. And then Principal LaRue would dock my pay. I'm not going to the poorhouse because of your carelessness," he said, and he pointed at the door. "You march yourself down to the nurse's office right this instant!" He fished a handkerchief out of his pocket and covered his nose and mouth.

Sabrina gathered her books into her backpack and slouched out of the classroom. As the door closed behind her she could hear the class break into a round of applause. *Should I hang a sign around my neck saying "Sick witch"?*

For that matter, what good would it do Sabrina to see the nurse, anyway? What could a woman who, by law and insurance codes, couldn't dispense anything stronger than a pat on the back do about a magical disease that stripped witches of their powers?

I can't imagine life without my powers anymore, thought Sabrina. *No more instant-delivery deluxe pizza, no more makeup-in-a-moment, and no more infinite wardrobe.* Then she remembered Drell. *Maybe no more me!* There was no question about it—she had to track down who had her powers. *What do I do first, wander the halls looking for loose magic?*

Nothing else came to mind, so Sabrina decided to wander the halls looking for signs of unusual . . . activity. She prowled the ground-floor corridors first, carefully avoiding the hall monitors. The student cops all too often thought of themselves as the enforcers of law and order in the entire school. If one of them caught her, Sabrina could legally say that she was headed for the nurse's office, but she was afraid that the officious student would insist on escorting her there.

The hallway of the school had deeply recessed windows lining the wall away from the class-rooms, looking out over the semi-enclosed area behind the school and the playing fields beyond. Sabrina scuttled from window bay to window bay, peering around the corner of each to make sure that the coast was clear.

She was approaching the gym, which was going to be a risky run. The gymnasium was two stories tall and occupied a hundred feet of hall-way. There were only two doorways to duck into for all that length, and Sabrina was sure that she'd get spotted before she made it through.

She hugged the corner of the window bay, judging her chances. Suddenly, a movement outside the window caught her attention. *Ohmigosh,* she thought. *I don't believe it!*

Heedless of detection now, Sabrina raced down the hall, past the gym, toward the double doors that opened to the rear of the school.

Bursting through the doors, she rounded the corner of the building at a dead run, then stopped short as the whole scene in front of her became clear.

Harvey sat beneath the oak in the Angle, his arms outstretched and his eyes huge with amazement. Dozens of birds were sitting on him! Robins jostled with jays for shoulder room, starlings hopped around on his head, and little finches lined up in neat rows along his arms, all looking raptly up at Harvey's face.

But the birds held only the ringside seats. Clustered around Harvey, almost filling the entire space of the Angle, sat more wildlife than Sabrina would have imagined lived in Westbridge. Gophers, moles, raccoons, badgers, and the like she might have expected, but full-grown wolves? And that bear couldn't have gotten that big eating the trash of suburbia!

Sabrina's skidding arrival spooked some of the birds, who burst into excited flight, shaking loose feathers as they flew. A piece of fluff settled on Sabrina's nose and she had an instant to stare at it with crossed eyes before a sneeze blew it away.

Chapter 5

Harvey was still slack-jawed with equal parts amazement and delight as he and Sabrina worked their way upstream through the departing students in the hall. "That was *incredible!*" Harvey kept repeating, each time with a little more emphasis.

"Easy for you to say," mumbled Sabrina. She dabbed at her drippy nose with a tissue in one hand and brushed feathers out of her blond hair with the other. "You weren't the one who was stampeded by the road company of *Bambi!*"

The student body of Westbridge High surged through the hallways like an amoeba, pulsing and shoving its way out of school and back into the outside world. It segmented and divided into groups that organized themselves and oriented toward different destinations. The vast majority

46

siphoned themselves onto buses that bore them away, dribbling them out on street corners and wooded roads.

Other groups filtered into the gym or out onto the fields, there to cluster around balls of various sizes. The group claiming the faculty of the school fragmented the most, squeezing singly into cars, although sharing the same dreams of loosened shoes, decent food, and quiet places that advertised instant attitude adjustment.

Buffeted by this dispersing organism, Harvey and Sabrina threaded their way toward the auditorium to become part of a brand-new blob of people—the hopeful applicants to the Westbridge High School Thespian Society.

"You go in first," suggested Harvey. "I need a minute by myself to get into my reading."

Sabrina was scrabbling around in her bag, pawing though crumpled tissues in search of an unused one. The itch in her nose had returned. "That's okay," she replied. "I have to paper . . . er, powder my nose." She ignored Harvey's puzzled look and broke for the girls' room.

Sabrina stuck out a hand to push the door open, then stopped in mid-gesture. She didn't want to bang into Jenny again, or anyone else, for that matter. Slowly, carefully, she grasped the handle and pulled it. To her surprise, the door didn't budge. Sabrina pulled harder. There was some response from the door, but still that stubborn resistance. Sabrina jerked at the door, throwing her strength into it. It flew open and Libby Chessler came staggering out, her hand still gripping the inner handle.

Sabrina jumped back as the cheerleader fell to the floor, her purse spilling its contents across the linoleum tiles. Plastic tubes of gloss and compacts skittered away to the sound of breaking glass. A strong floral scent rose in a cloying cloud, inflaming the itch in Sabrina's nose.

"You clumsy freak!" Libby snarled. She clutched a raw silk dressing gown around her as she bent to pick up her fashion first-aid kit. "What are you doing in here, anyway? I distinctly told you to use the freaks' bathroom."

Sabrina ignored her and rushed to the sink, tugging tissue from a dispenser. *I can't sneeze! No matter what, I can't sneeze,* she moaned to herself. *Not here! Not now!* Libby's perfume was making it a tough fight, though. In desperation, she tore a tissue in half and wadded the pieces up her nose.

Libby gawked in horror. "What are you doing? Is that some sort of strange freak ritual?" In a panic, she swept all of her cosmetics into her bag without looking and backed toward the door. "Don't come near me! I know all about your kind. I read about it in the *Weekly Inquiring News.*"

Sabrina clenched her hands, her nails biting into her palms, resisting with all her might the need to sneeze. Just as Libby reached the door, the need passed. Sabrina relaxed.

And then she sneezed. A tiny little thing, barely strong enough to pop the wadded tissues out of her nose. But it was enough. Sabrina felt the tingle of her powers leaving just as Libby opened the door and left the room.

When Sabrina entered the auditorium there were a dozen or more people milling about, waiting for Mrs. Bozigian to arrive and get things started. The auditorium was a small affair, little more than an extra-deep classroom with a stage. An upright piano stood to one side, just in front of an American flag, the gold on its eagle looking just a bit tarnished. Harvey sat on the piano bench, his back to the keyboard. Libby slinked nearby, artfully draping her silk sleeves over his shoulders as she passed.

Jenny strolled up to Sabrina, but stopped a careful four feet from her. "Some turnout, eh?" She seemed to be trying to strike a balance between wary friendliness and exaggerated self-preservation. "Did you pick a reading yet?"

Sabrina did a double take. It had completely slipped her mind! "Ah . . . no. What are you going to do?"

"Queen Lear, by William Shakespeare," Jenny said with pride.

"Queen *Lear?"*

"Yeah," enthused Jenny. "You see, by transforming the patriarchal structure of the play into a matriarchal one, I can illuminate and share the oppression of women in the subtext."

"I can feel the oppression already," grimaced Sabrina. Harvey walked up to join them, but stopped at about the same distance from Sabrina that Jenny had. "What are you going to do?" Sabrina asked him.

Harvey grinned sheepishly, but his answer was cut short by another voice.

"Populist trash," sneered Libby, who had followed Harvey across the room. "I'm going to perform an interpretation of one of the greatest American showpieces." She whipped off her silk dressing gown, flinging it dramatically onto a row of chairs. Beneath it, Libby wore a tight spandex outfit spray-painted with the intricate multicolored pattern of a calico cat's fur. A collar of fluffy faux fur, painted gloves, and a long, calico-colored tail filled out the costume. Libby brushed her hands back over her hair and set a barrette with large cat ears on her head. She pawed the air before her dramatically. "I'm doing Grizabella," she purred.

Jenny was incensed. Her pale skin flushed a companion pink under her red hair. "Hey, that's not a reading! All she did was sing!"

"And *Cats* was a British play," Sabrina pointed out.

"It was a hit on Broadway, wasn't it?" Libby retorted smugly. "That's American."

Sabrina felt miserable enough to tell the truth directly for a change. "Why don't you try competing on an even field for once?"

Libby looked puzzled, as if the idea had never occurred to her before. Then she shrugged, dismissing the notion, and sneered. "I don't need to. That would be stooping. Besides, I'm sophomore class president. I should have preference."

Jenny snorted. "Sorry, but the last time I looked, this was still a democracy."

"So? I'm not going to let a little thing like that hold me back," Libby replied archly. Her mood soured at being challenged by these social outcasts. "I don't have to put up with this," she pouted darkly. She pointed a finger imperiously at Sabrina and Jenny. "I'll get in, and I *won't* have to read."

Sabrina barely had time to notice the light tingling of the spell that Libby was unknowingly casting as Mrs. Bozigian, the home economics teacher, bustled into the room. With her hair done up in neat cornrows and sparkling beads, she had the air of Martha Stewart, emulating the same ultra-efficient style.

"Welcome, welcome, fellow devotees of the thespian arts. Thank you all for expressing your interest in our little theatrical endeavor." A couple of students blinked in confusion, already lost by Mrs. Bozigian's profuse style. "This will be a day that will long live in your memories, perhaps to pass along to your future grandchildren—the founding of the Westbridge High School Thespian Society, destined to take its place amid the hallowed ranks of the Actor's Studio, the Circle in the Square, and the Westbridge Dinner Theater, which I happen to direct."

"Isn't that a little ambitious for high school?" Harvey whispered to Sabrina.

"Let her dream," she replied in an undertone. "We'll be out of here in three years. She's gonna stay forever."

Mrs. Bozigian ran her eyes over the assembled students, beaming in pleasure at the sight. Under her scrutiny, the students straightened up and Libby preened, licking at a paw and smoothing her fur. "You'll all have a wonderful time, I'm sure. As soon as you all sign the extracurricular activity sheet by the door, we'll begin with our first acting exercises."

"Excuse me, Mrs. B.," Harvey spoke hesitantly. "Weren't we supposed to prepare a reading for auditions?"

Mrs. Bozigian looked briefly confused. "Not that I recall, Harvey."

Jenny chimed in. "But you specifically told us to read."

"Nonsense. I probably said that I'd give you a lot *to* read, and you misunderstood me."

So this is how it looks from the outside, thought Sabrina. She knew very well why Mrs. Bozigian didn't remember asking the students to prepare a reading. Libby's spell had wiped it from the teacher's mind so that Libby wouldn't be bothered with having to read. Sabrina glanced at the cheerleader, expecting to see her wearing an expression of smug triumph.

Instead, Libby looked like she was about to have a snit. "Excuse me?" she snapped. "Are you saying that all these wanna-bes are in? Automatically?"

"Why, of course, dear," replied Mrs. Bozigian. "This is a democracy, after all, and the blessings of theater should be shared by—"

"Why do people keep saying that like it's some kind of reason for things not being the way I want them? I mean, what's the point of being special if everyone gets the same privileges?" Libby stood up. "I'm sorry . . . I have better things to do than this. And if I don't, I'll create them." She whisked her dressing gown up from the chair and glided out like a feline empress making a recession.

"Too bad. Now who will we cast for the Wicked Witch of the West?" cracked Sabrina automatically. Then she suddenly realized: *Witch? Libby just left the room with my powers!* She broke for the door.

"Are you too good for us, too, Miss Spellman?" Mrs. Bozigian asked, barely masking the hurt in her voice. "Are you leaving as well?"

"Yes! I mean, no . . . I, uh . . ." Sabrina stopped as she groped for an answer. "I'm going to see if I can talk Libby into hanging around." She fled the room before the teacher could reply.

The delay in getting out of the auditorium was short, but it was long enough to doom Sabrina. She got to the front doors of the school just in time to see Libby climb into a taxi and roar away.

Great! Now Libby's conjuring up cabs in Westbridge! she thought. *What's next?*

Chapter 6

☆

Libby climbed out of the yellow taxi at the main entrance to Westbridge Mall. The driver held out her credit card and a pen. Libby grabbed them, scrawled her name on the driver's fare sheet, and practically threw them back at him. As she stomped into the mall, the taxi burned rubber as it tore away from the curb, wrapping her in a cloud of greasy fumes that made her cough. He must have discovered there was no tip added to his fare. Libby had never understood the need to tip service people—weren't they already being paid to do their jobs?

Snarling, she flapped her dressing gown to clear the air, then pushed through the glass doors to enter the mall. Forgetting that she was still in a *Cats* costume, she was caught up short when the automatic doors closed on her tail. She muttered rude words under her breath as she angrily yanked at it, freeing it at the expense of half its faux fur.

If there was one thing Libby Chessler hated more than anything else in the world, it was frustration. Today had been one frustration after another, starting with that upstart little blonde, Sabrina Spellman. Frustrations like that could be soothed only by intensive shopping. Libby maneuvered her way through the mall at a brisk pace, ignoring the people who stopped to stare at her unusual shopping attire, and headed right into Daddy's Money, the closest thing to an exclusive boutique that Westbridge had.

She raked her way through a selection of smart outfits hanging from a rack made of chromed and welded farm implements. With expert skill she flipped past hanger after hanger, yanking some up to add to the pile draped over her left arm, and leaving the rest in disarray. When she had collected seven or eight possibilities, Libby walked toward the dressing room.

Before she reached the room's doorway, the shopgirl stepped in front of her. "I'm sorry, Miss. You can't take more than three items into the changing room at once." The shopgirl was young, barely out of high school, and nervous about having to be a disciplinarian.

"Excuse me?" Libby wilted her with a serpentine stare. "Are you looking to blow your commission?" When the cowed girl made no answer, Libby pushed past her toward the little cubicle.

Libby sneered as she jammed her selections onto the single hook on the wall. There were such poor pickings to be had here! Just three Ralph Lauren designs and only one Liz Claiborne. Everything else in the store was from nobodies. Ah, well, maybe a shopping trip to Boston was in order this weekend.

One by one, Libby tried the outfits on, and one by one she tossed them carelessly on the bench. She hated them all. But there was no way she was going to leave Daddy's Money without buying something. She started picking up pieces of the different outfits, matching this and that, and holding each combination up to the mirror for inspection.

Soon the hangers on the hook were empty, and Libby had made a combination that looked halfway decent. Well, at least no one else in school would have one like it. She looked at her reflection in the mirror critically.

She had settled on a scarlet leather skirt and a vest that matched, sort of. It had lots of extra straps and zippers and made a faint clinking sound when it moved that was guaranteed to attract attention. But the color was off, and the straps didn't fit her figure well.

Under the vest was a silk blouse with a stiff, open collar flaring into rounded points and long, tight sleeves. An amber pendant picked up the burnt sienna color of her stockings. Her feet were bare; shoes would have to wait.

Libby frowned into the mirror, annoyed at how lopsided the vest looked on her. Why couldn't they make clothes that fit better than this? She certainly paid enough for them. And the alterations wouldn't be that hard. She pointed at the errant straps in the mirror. All that had to be done was to move *that* one up an inch and take *that* seam in. . . .

When Sabrina's aunts had begun giving her instructions on casting spells, they had started with the simplest of commands: concentrate and point. Libby's strongest asset was her concentration. She was wonderfully focused on herself and her desires. She always knew exactly what she wanted and, usually, how to get people to give it to her. And she was known throughout the school as an imperious pointer, given the constant parade of classmates worth ridiculing.

That combination was enough to kick her new magic powers into gear. The straps of her vest suddenly shifted upward all on their own. The seams tightened and the garish color mellowed. The vest now fit perfectly.

Libby's mouth dropped open in shock.

Libby, being Libby, immediately assumed that someone was tricking her. "Who's doing this?" she demanded of the booth, looking at the ceiling and walls for a camera or a peephole. "I could have you arrested and sent to jail for spying on me! My daddy knows lots of hungry lawyers!"

Finding no telltale holes or lenses in the walls, she turned her attention back to the mirror. The culprit was probably hiding behind two-way glass. She pointed an accusing finger at the glass and commanded, "Let's just see what's behind that mirror."

Before she could grab the frame of the mirror and pull on it, however, the whole glass simply lifted off the wall and floated off to one side. The wall behind the mirror was blank, if a little cleaner than the rest of the dressing room. There was no hidden camera crew trying to assemble a "Libby Chessler at her worst" video to embarrass her at school.

Libby was so caught in her fury at thinking she was being spied on that it took a full moment for her attention to return to the mirror—the one that was floating in midair six inches away from the wall. The impossibility of it all suddenly crashed into her brain, and without her attention and focus to keep it levitated, the mirror crashed, too.

The sound of shattering glass in the small dressing room was louder than Libby could ever have imagined. Each shard hitting the floor was an accusation that made her flinch. From beyond the door came a muffled, "Are you all right in there, Miss?"

Libby couldn't answer. How was she ever

going to get out of this mess without being humiliated or cut to ribbons? If there was one thing Libby hated more than frustration, it was humiliation. If the management of Daddy's Money saw this mess, Libby would never be able to face them again. That meant no real shopping except on trips to Boston! All Libby wanted in the world at that moment was for the mirror to be whole and hanging on the wall again.

She glared at the glittering fragments on the floor. "You floated and broke all by yourself," she hissed, shaking a finger at the mess. "Why can't you just fix yourself, too?"

In a blink, every fragment of glass leaped into the air. The mirror reassembled itself and hung itself back in its proper place, whole and perfect, with not a crack or mar to accuse her. Libby stared mutely at the miracle.

Jingling keys unlocked the cubicle door. The manager, a stocky pudding of a man who was clearly uncomfortable violating a female dressing room, leaned hesitantly in. The timid shopgirl peeped nervously around his shoulder. The manager harrumphed at Libby and asked, "Is everything okay, ma'am?"

Libby summoned her most regal stare. "Of course," she said, batting her eyes at the manager. "Why shouldn't it be?" She ripped the tags off the various parts of her outfit and held them out. "Charge these to my account like a dear fellow, would you?"

The manager accepted the tags but took a few seconds to look around the cubicle. His lips pursed at the sight of Libby's crumpled reject pile, but no comment escaped them. He smiled insincerely at Libby, backed out of the dressing room, and closed the door. A heated argument conducted in whispers receded down the hall.

Libby slumped onto the bench to regroup. What had just gone on here? She stared intently at the mirror. Had her mind snapped or—

—or had her mind somehow progressed to that higher level that all her self-help books always talked about?

Libby Chessler owned the town's largest collection of self-help and self-modification books. Not those whiny, "why am I such a loser?" books. Hers all had titles like *Winning Through Intimidation, Overachieve Now!, Cheerleaders Uber Alles,* and her latest, *Visualize!—The Power to Mentally Dominate Your World.*

This last book promised that if the buyer imagined what she wanted clearly enough and commanded it to happen, her higher level would kick in and make it happen. These books usually prescribed their techniques for managing difficult life goals—things like getting promotions, winning business deals, and dating. But Libby couldn't recall them ever saying anything about levitating mirrors.

"Make it work now and understand it later" seemed to be an appropriate working method for her. "You want to be a magic mirror?" she challenged the fixture. "Let's put you through your paces." She pointed at it and commanded, "Show me something that will make me happy!"

Ripples pulsed across the surface of the mirror, distorting Libby's reflection. As the rings reached the frame they rebounded and collided with oncoming waves. Libby's image broke up into fragments as the rings atomized. The rippling slowed, and the image came back. Well, *an* image, that is. Instead of reflecting Libby, the mirror showed a glum and bedraggled Sabrina Spellman slumped in a booth at the Slicery. Sabrina looked sick and miserable.

"That's not what I thought I'd get," mused Libby. "But since this day is mostly her fault, it does make me happier to know she's suffering, too." She pondered a moment, deciding on what question to ask next.

Some of her books claimed that supernatural helpers were responsible for shifting the odds in the book buyer's favor. Was that the source of her sudden power? Libby looked around nervously. Was there an invisible watcher lurking around? The thought of an unseen helper watching her every move made Libby's flesh creep. She had to know. She pointed. "Mirror! Show me the source of my powers!"

The image in the mirror stayed the same. Libby smacked the frame as if it were a malfunctioning vending machine. "Do what I told you!"

she snapped angrily. The image stayed the same, with only the people moving around behind Sabrina changing. "Okay, so what has this got to do with my higher level?" she whined.

The scene in the mirror suddenly spun away from Sabrina and zipped out of the Slicery, tearing along the streets of Westbridge at a reckless pace. In a moment, it made a wide turn at the corner of Collins Street and stopped before number 133. It paused long enough for Libby to recognize the Spellmans' old Victorian house before it zoomed forward, passing *through* the door and up the grand staircase to the second floor. A quick zigzag along the hall and then *through* another door brought the image to rest in front of a large book labeled *The Discovery of Magic*.

Libby stared at the massive book in awe and envy. She'd never seen *that* self-help book before, not in Westbridge, not even in Boston. She was on the mailing lists of dozens of self-improvement catalogs, and even they didn't offer anything remotely like it. From the look of the leatherwork and the jewels adorning the cover, it was obviously a pricey limited edition.

Libby was confused. How did a nobody like Sabrina rate such an exclusive prize? The confusion deepened to anger. If Sabrina had this power, then the humiliations Libby had often suffered suddenly had a reason. Libby was a top cheerleader. She knew how envy worked.

Her mind cleared. Now that she had an opponent, all of Libby's instincts and training kicked into gear. After all, there could be only one Number One in any contest, and second place was really the first loser. But how was she going to learn the secrets of that book? It was a cinch that Sabrina wouldn't loan her the book for extended study. She needed a copy of her own.

Libby stared at the image in the mirror, all thoughts of shopping banished. All she needed was a peek at the title page of that book, to see who the publisher was. Then she could order her own, if necessary, getting some strings pulled to make it happen. But how was she going to get that peek?

Well, her higher level should know, shouldn't it? She faced the mirror and commanded, "What do I need to do to get to that book?"

Nothing happened. Libby almost panicked. Had she lost IT already? What had she done wrong? Quickly, she reviewed how the mirror had originally come to life and shown her things. First, she had pointed at the mirror, then yelled . . .

Pointing! That was it. Libby pointed a French-wrapped index nail at the mirror and intoned, "What do I need to do to get to that book?" She sounded like some schmaltzy dinner-theater gypsy, but it seemed to do the job.

The image in the mirror shifted back to a reflection of Libby in the dressing room. Slowly and deliberately, the Libby in the mirror morphed into Sabrina Spellman—a Sabrina who turned and walked into the Spellman house like she lived there.

"You mean I have to become Sabrina?" Libby was repulsed. "Ewww." How could she impersonate someone so totally uncool? Wouldn't her natural hipness leak through and betray her? "You're sure I have to?" she demanded of the girl in the mirror. The image nodded. "And you can do this for me?" Again the nod.

Libby jabbed at the mirror and ordered, "Do it!"

The mousy shopgirl, whose name was Phoebe, hovered around the doorway to the dressing area, though she never actually set foot in the corridor beyond. She had an uneasy feeling about that snooty girl in the changing room. Phoebe *had* heard breaking glass in there, no matter what the manager said after he'd shut the door. And now she was going to prove that this—she looked down at the charge slip in her hand—*Libby Chessler* was trying to pull some sort of scam.

The problem was, people like Libby Chessler scared Phoebe. She wilted before their self-confidence, their self-assurance drawing strength out of her and collapsing her like an emptied shell. It was like they had secret powers just because they were right all the time.

That's how Phoebe figured they did it. Being right made you strong, and then being strong made you righter. Or more right—however those smart high school kids would say it. It was a loop, and Phoebe knew that she could do it, too, if she could start out being right about something.

Phoebe mustered her courage and crossed the doorway. She tiptoed down the corridor and stopped outside the closed dressing room door. If she could figure out what this Chessler girl was up to and expose her, that just could be her leg up to success. She leaned her head against the door, listening.

The door swung open suddenly, smacking Phoebe in the head and sending her reeling. When the stars cleared from her head, she saw the red outfit that the Chessler girl had worn walking away down the corridor. Only now there was a petite blonde in the outfit, not a sullen brunette. Phoebe yelled at the retreating figure, "Hey! Come back here! Those aren't your clothes!" It was the most forceful thing she'd ever said.

To Phoebe's absolute shock and surprise, the girl stopped and turned to face her. "Ex-*cuse* me?" the blonde answered frostily. "Do you have a problem?"

Phoebe seized her courage with both hands. There was something seriously wrong here. Normally, she'd call for the manager to handle it, but her ears were still ringing from the chewing out he'd given her after the broken-glass false alarm. She decided to handle the situation herself. "Those-clothes-were-paid-for-by-someone-else-and-you're-not-her!" she bleated. Phoebe took a deep breath to calm herself. "You'll have to wait here until Security comes."

A look of sudden irritation crossed the blonde's face. She pointed a regal finger at Phoebe and hissed, "You have no idea who you're dealing with."

Suddenly Phoebe realized that the blonde was right. She *had* no idea who the person standing before her was. Stare as hard as she might, Phoebe couldn't figure out who she was—or what she was doing there. In the back of her mind, she knew that something out of line was happening, but the more she struggled with it, the less she knew about it. In an instant, her mind was empty, completely unaware of why she was standing in the dressing room corridor in front of a total stranger.

"May I help you?" she asked in her normal mousy voice.

The blonde looked at her suspiciously. "You're not going to call Security?"

"Goodness me, no," Phoebe said. "Why, is something wrong?"

A slow, smug smile crept over the blonde's face. "No . . . ." she replied slowly, ". . . nothing's wrong. In fact, things are exceptionally *good.*"

She did an about-face and strode confidently out of the store.

Phoebe watched her leave, a nagging itch in the back of her mind trying to tell her something. As she shook her head to clear it, she saw the scattered clothing in the fitting room and sighed in dismay. Another mess for her to clean up. She started picking up clothes, wondering who had come in here and gone on a fashion rampage. For the life of her, she couldn't remember having had a customer in hours.

Chapter 7

Libby hated Sabrina's body from the moment she assumed it. She couldn't quite identify why. Her mind knew how to walk, talk, and act cool, but when she did it in this body, those reflexes felt stiff and unnatural. Besides, Sabrina was a freak. Even though it was genuine Libby inside this body, people might not realize that and treat her like a freak. Nobody would ever get away with treating Libby Chessler like a freak.

She came to a halt outside the mall, suddenly struck by the problem of getting to Sabrina's house without being spotted. She didn't dare walk through town for fear that someone would approach her, thinking she was actually Sabrina—or worse, somehow meet the real Sabrina. Libby knew from her magic mirror that Sabrina was presently moping in the Slicery, over by the school. She had only a short time to act if she was to pull this impersonation off without getting caught.

As she stood there, a taxi cruising for fares drove slowly by the mall entrance. Reflexively, Libby waved a hand and hailed the cab.

"Where to, babe?" the driver, a short, stocky man with an air of permanent disgruntlement, asked insolently. Ordinarily, Libby would have automatically ripped into anyone who dared to call her "babe," but was caught off guard by the sudden need to remember Sabrina's address.

"One thirty-three Collins Street," she said after a moment's frantic racking of her memory. Libby knew the addresses of every mover and shaker in Westbridge, but had never bothered to pay attention to where nonentities lived. Although she had seen Sabrina's house enough to know that she lived in it, if it weren't for the magic-mirror routine, she would never have known the address.

The sticky floor of the cab's backseat reminded Libby in no uncertain terms that she'd forgotten to get shoes for this outfit. She had stuffed all of her school clothes into her locker before changing into her costume, and had left the Thespian Society meeting in such a huff that she'd ignored her shoeless condition.

Libby stared at her finger in sudden inspiration—why not see just how much her higher level could deliver. She pointed the finger at her feet and muttered, "Gucci's. Red leather."

"You say somethin'?" called the driver over his shoulder.

"Not to you," snapped Libby, staring at the boots that had appeared on her feet. They were the right color and style, but she had never heard of designer boots called "Gookies" before. And why was their logo a face sticking its tongue out under a mop of curly pink hair?

"Nice outfit, sweetheart," commented the driver, staring at Libby in the rearview mirror. "Not like the clown I had in here before ya. She was a sight, I'll tellya. Looked like she walked straight outta the circus."

Recognition dawned on Libby as she glared at the driver's reflection. She had wound up in the same taxi that had taken her to the mall. That meant that he was talking about . . . "For your information, that was a costume from *Cats*," she retorted archly.

"It was a costume from Goodwill, if ya ask me. Chick never checked out what she looked like. With all that fluff and fuzz, she was more like a canary with measles, I say. Mostly 'cause she was cheep." He laughed heartily at his own joke. "She didn't leave me a tip, so she's cheap. Cheep, cheep, get it?"

"I get it, all right," Libby snarled under her breath. "And you will, too, if you keep it up."

"Here's yer stop, lady," the driver announced as he pulled up in front of the Spellman house. "That'll be two-fifty. Plus tip," he added pointedly.

Libby clambered out of the cab, her new boots feeling stiff and clunky. "I need you to wait for me. I'll only be a few minutes."

"Right. I wait here and you skip out and stiff me for the fare. I been around once or twice, ya know."

"But you're going to have to take the time to fix those flats, anyway," Libby said innocently.

"What flats?"

"Those flats," she said, jabbing a finger at the two passenger-side tires. The tires obediently deflated with a whoosh. "I'll probably be back before you're done." In fact, Libby knew she would, because she had specifically visualized tires with unpatchable holes.

She left the driver staring at the two useless tires and cursing a blue streak as she walked up to the massive front door of the Spellman house.

One thirty-three Collins Street was an imposing old Queen Anne tower-style Victorian house. The tower that gave the style its name squatted at the right corner of the structure, anchoring it in an off-center fashion. In a way, it looked like a slightly confused matron, surrounded by her peers on the block but not quite caught up in time.

Gables flanked the tower, each with its own eccentric scrollwork. Overhead, weathered shingles made a faded coiffure, while, lower down, the sprawling veranda splayed like a white-painted hoopskirt with its skirts half-lifted. The whole effect was one of bemused gentility, welcoming but turning a blind eye to the modern or unpleasant.

Libby walked resolutely up the steps of the veranda entranceway. At the oak door with the etched glass panes, she almost stopped and knocked before remembering that she *was* Sabrina now. As far as anyone knew, she belonged here.

Libby tried the knob and was surprised to feel it turn under her hand. The big door swung open at a touch. On reconsideration, the unlocked door seemed less unusual. Westbridge was still a small enough community that many people didn't feel the need to lock their doors. Just to be safe, however, Libby called out loudly as she stepped inside, "Hi—I'm home."

No voice answered her. The house was quiet. The only sound reaching her ears came from the damask curtains rustling in front of open windows. It was cool but light inside, the afternoon sun filtering in through pastel sheers. Everywhere was warm wood and comfortable fabric, snug wainscoting and tasteful wallpaper.

To her left, Libby could see a sort of library or sitting room, with deep, comfy-looking chairs beneath rank after rank of old books in cases. To her right, there was a living room, with a couch-

and-chairs conversation grouping and a grand piano in the tower window bay beyond.

And directly in front of her, just as the mirror had shown her, was a broad walnut staircase leading up to the second floor. Libby walked softly over to the stairs and ascended quietly, senses pitched to detect the slightest hint of another person in the house. Libby didn't know what the Spellman sisters did for a living, but it was apparent they weren't home now. It seemed deserted, but that wouldn't last. She had to move quickly.

The creepiness of prowling around someone else's house grew inside her. Suddenly she desperately wanted to hear spy music. Every spy movie Libby had ever seen had background music for times like these. It kept you on your toes and, if the strings jittered nervously, warned you of danger ahead.

She made it to the landing without hearing violins cry *scree scree scree,* and paused to take her bearings. There, around to the right, was where Sabrina's bedroom should be. Libby pushed the door open and gasped a little to actually see the book the mirror had promised was the key to higher powers.

It sat on a tall bookstand of carved dark wood. There were gems set in its cover and a heavy silk bookmark threaded through the parchment pages. The cover itself was made of fine dark leather, tooled with strange and eccentric

.designs—symbols or glyphs from some forgotten language. Libby approached and ran her hands over it.

Raised gilt letters read *The Discovery of Magic*. Libby snorted scornfully. Not only was Sabrina a freak, but she was an insane freak. Did she really think that she was a witch? She must have accidentally invoked her higher level and then mistook its effects for magic.

On the other hand, Libby's higher level had indicated that this book was necessary for understanding and controlling Libby's new powers. Libby *never* passed up an opportunity to work out new ways of controlling power. She would probably have to skim the whole book to find the one or two nuggets of useful information buried in all that witch nonsense. And since there was no telling when Sabrina or her aunts would be home, she'd better start skimming.

Libby opened the heavy volume to the page that was bookmarked, figuring that to be as good a place as any to start reading. Both sides of the spread were covered with dense writing in a crabbed printing, interspersed with diagrams or line engravings. On the top of the right-hand page was a box labeled WITCH DOCTOR. In the center of that box was a drawing of a hand-lettered note. The note read "THE DOCTOR IS OUT."

"Stupid jokes? This is a book with stupid jokes?" Libby poked at the illustration with a finger. To her surprise, a bodiless voice spoke from thin air.

"I'm sorry, I'm out of the book right now, but if you leave a message, I'll get back to you when I get off the green. If you are Sabrina Spellman calling, please fill out these forms and stick them into the binding."

A stack of paperwork slid out of what Libby would have sworn was a straight ink line on the page. It landed with a plop on the floor. She scooped it up reflexively and read the top page.

BLUE CAULDRON INSURANCE CO. HMO

HEALERS AND METAPHYSICIANS ORGANIZATION

Maintaining paranormal powers for 10,000 years

PATIENT: Spellman, Sabrina, Ms.

COMPLAINT: Sneezing, running nose, loss of witch-powers.

DIAGNOSIS: Spellfluenza infestation, contagious, 24-hour variety.

TREATMENT: Avoid all mortal contact for 24 hours.

Please sign in triplicate and return to your local Blue Cauldron HMO office.

Libby set the papers down slowly, stunned by the revelation. She had been wrong. Completely wrong. It took a lot for a supremely popular person to admit that.

The strange powers she had been suddenly gifted with did not come from a higher level, no matter what her self-improvement books said. They were supernatural powers. And that meant that while Sabrina Spellman was still a freak, she wasn't an insane freak. She really *was* a witch. Which explained a lot of strange things that had gone on since Sabrina had transferred to Westbridge High School.

For one thing, it explained how a nobody like Sabrina could flaunt Libby's master plan to use school as a testing ground for social control. Being head cheerleader and president of the sophomore class were only the beachhead of a strategy of manipulation and ambition that would one day take her to the White House . . . or beyond. All the students were supposed to neatly line up behind Libby or be condemned to suffer the agonies of outsiderhood, like that Kelly girl or that geek Gordie. It was unnatural that Sabrina, having been certified by Libby as an outsider, should have managed to organize those hopeless dregs of school society and give them a sense of self-respect that they should have only gotten by following Libby, and at her whim.

This was the answer then. And if it was something Sabrina could do, then it was certain that Libby could. In fact, it was something Libby *had* to do, like the sun had to rise each day and a new set of fashions had to appear quarterly—it was the natural order of things.

Libby closed the massive book, lifted it from its stand, and carried it over to Sabrina's desk. No thought of danger or interruption entered her mind. Her only interest now was to examine this book and learn as much about her new powers as she could.

Chapter 8

The Slicery was a comfortable, hole-in-the-wall pizza joint in a court just off the street that led to the high school. Like most New England business buildings, it was made of sturdy brick, and had housed many different shops and businesses before being transformed into the focus of off-campus life. There were even picturesque chips and holes that tradition maintained were scars the structure had suffered during the Revolutionary War. Those of the more poetic and contemplative bent claimed that if one sat quietly, one could feel the weight of history within the rough brick walls.

Not that anyone in the Slicery came there for peace and quiet. With a jukebox, three video games, a Foosball table, a pinball machine, taped music, loud conversation, and shouted pizza orders, the place was more pumped adrenaline than laid-back.

The usual after-school crowd was there, unwinding from school, postponing as long as possible the return to their own homes, just hanging out, and watching and being watched. There were jocks in their jerseys, fresh from practice or skipping out of practice, the entire lower-grade "soph" set, intent on impressing themselves and anyone around them with their practiced looks of sophistication and the latest styles copied from *Seventeen, YM,* and *'Teen.*

The same rules about seating and association applied to the Slicery as much as the cafeteria, but there was room for mingling here. In fact, admiring or envious younger crowds were necessary in order for the upperclassmen to feel properly superior. Had Mr. Pool been aware that the Slicery existed, he would have certainly had a field day taking notes for a paper on pizza joints as laboratories for perfecting human pecking orders.

In the middle of all this pheromone-soaked bustle, Sabrina sat surrounded by a zone of funk, brooding over the day's events. It wasn't fair that her life had flown out the window with a mere sneeze. She dreaded going home. How could she explain things to her aunts? Or Drell.

Harvey kept trying to cheer her up, hovering

solicitously, offering to fetch pizza or soda, hinting at how much fun a game of Foosball might be. But Sabrina was too low to pay much attention to his attempts at comforting. How could he comfort her? She couldn't even tell him what was really wrong. How could he believe that Sabrina was not only a witch, but a witch clumsy enough to lose her powers to a cheerleader?

And what was Libby doing with Sabrina's powers right now? Libby might be selfish, supercilious, and callous, but no one had ever taken her for dumb. Sooner or later she would do something magical and realize that she had a chance at real power. The thought of Libby with power made her shiver.

So threatening was this image that it pulled Sabrina up enough to notice Harvey sitting with her. He was chewing pizza with his eyes closed, his body bopping to the beat of the background music. He was the perfect picture of normalcy. Sabrina decided to ask him for a reality check.

"Harvey," she began, "I've got a really odd question for you. Not a this-is-something-that-could-really-happen-and-I'd-feel-responsible kind of question. I'm just curious, honest." Harvey opened his eyes and looked directly at Sabrina. "What do you think Libby would do if she suddenly had unlimited power?"

Harvey grinned wryly. "You mean, she doesn't? She's captain of the cheerleading squad and class president already."

"I mean beyond that." Something in Sabrina's tone made Harvey seriously ponder.

"Well, she's sixteen," he said, screwing up his face in thought, "so that rules out the White House for a while. I suppose she would want to be a movie star or Donald Trump's new ex-wife. Something where everybody would look up to her and do what she told them to."

"Oh, good. That's a relief." Sabrina slumped back down on the table.

Harvey was confused. "Whattaya mean, 'oh, good'?"

"I thought she might turn all blondes into frogs or something," Sabrina replied without lifting her head from her arms.

"Ahh, don't let her get to you. She's not some kind of monster, just the head cheerleader." Harvey finished his pizza in two enormous bites, daintily cramming the last bit of crust in his mouth with a finger. He crumpled his napkin into his paper plate, crushing both and arcing them into a trash can twenty feet away. The words "Doo boints!" fought their way out of his filled mouth.

"Thanks, that gives me lots of confidence in her moral fiber."

Harvey was determined to be cheerful. "You're just bummed 'cause of your cold. Let me walk you home so you can get some rest." He scooped up their jackets from the chair backs. "I could show you some great mailboxes on the way."

At that moment, Libby was sitting at Sabrina's desk, turning the pages of *The Discovery of Magic.* "It's about time you got home," a male voice said behind her. "There's hardly enough sun left to take a decent nap." Libby's heart stopped in her chest and she snapped around to see who had caught her. All she saw was a black Burmese cat lazily strolling toward the window seat. "Would you mind pulling the curtains open?" the cat clearly said. "You know how my claws snag so easily." The animal leaped up on the seat and threw himself down in the small shaft of sunlight that pierced the curtains.

"A talking cat. Giving me orders." Libby's shock was so deep that she was reduced to repeating the obvious in a monotone.

"Go ahead, rub it in," sniffed the cat. "I lost my witch-powers and got sentenced to a hundred years as a house cat. I suppose I deserve whatever mean things you want to say to me after this morning's little switcheroo."

"Witch-powers . . ." Sudden light was dawning in Libby's brain. She'd always heard stories about how traditional witches had familiars—spirits in animal form to advise them and do their bidding. This cat, or whatever-it-was-in-cat-form, must be Sabrina's familiar. But why wasn't he angry that Libby was in Sabrina's room? It took a moment for Libby to remember that she had let the magic mirror—or rather, her higher level—transform her into an exact duplicate of Sabrina.

The cat brightened as a thought struck him. "Of course, if you *do* feel the need to sneeze in my presence, I'll take better care of your powers this time, I promise. No more fish. Well, maybe a little caviar." He jumped down from his perch and made a beeline for Libby's legs.

Libby may have had Sabrina's body, but her reflexes were all Libby Chessler, and Libby Chessler *hated* cats, Broadway hits or not. The second the Burmese brushed his fur against her skin, she flinched and yelped, "Get *away* from me!"

Salem was just leaning forward to rub along a leg when that leg jerked violently away, leaving him to tumble forward, off-balance. He had come close enough, however, for his senses to come into play. He arched his back at Libby and growled, "Hey! You're not Sabrina!"

Libby did a double take and then assumed an exaggeratedly relaxed pose in the chair. "How could you tell? I mean, what makes you say that?"

Salem sneered. "Sabrina smells like a nap in warm sunshine. You smell like a winter night on a cold stoop. Since I know of only one of Sabrina's schoolmates that fits that description, I presume you're that Libby person."

"I wouldn't talk about personal smells, Mr. Bathes-With-His-Tongue," retorted Libby. She shivered violently. "Eww—I can't even *think* of how gross that would be."

"Enough with the pleasant insults. What are you doing here, or is breaking-and-entering now part of cheerleaders' training? Along with magical impersonation, which I don't think the rule book addresses at all."

When push came to shove, Libby had always felt that the appropriate response was to shove back—hard. She drew herself up imperially and barked at the cat, "I'm here because your witch-freak owner has magic powers, which *I* now have and which I intend to *keep.*"

The reality of the situation finally sank into Salem's brain. It had taken a while, but a cat's brain *is* the size of a walnut, and some thought processes have to wait in line before getting their proper attention. "Uh-oh, we've got trouble here," he spat. He scrabbled for the door, yelling, "Zelda! Hilda!"

"Oh, no you don't!" shouted Libby, pointing a finger at the fleeing cat.

Libby's time alone with the book of magic hadn't been enough to do more than tempt her with the possibilities inherent in her powers, but she had a spiteful imagination combined with a great natural aptitude for giving orders. Simple thoughts and great power can accomplish for some what it normally takes practice and memorization to do.

In a flash, Salem was yanked up off the floor by invisible hands and sent flying toward the ceiling. He had no time to think about his reaction, but fortunately for him, his cat reflexes moved faster than his brain. When a cat is dropped from a height, he always lands feet-first. Salem discovered that applied to ceilings as well, if you're falling *up.*

Which is how he found himself hanging upside down from the ceiling of Sabrina's bedroom, his claws desperately imbedded in plaster and lath. He yowled with fear and stared down at his tormentor.

Libby sneered up at him. "That should keep you from causing any trouble until I'm done here. Now, I need some answers and you're going to give them to me."

Salem's characteristic sarcasm overrode his fear. He rolled his eyes and drawled, "Oh, right. What makes you think I'd help you?"

Libby flashed him a 100-watt threatening smile. "I have a witch's power. I have a book of spells, some of them *very* nasty if used the wrong way. And I don't like cats."

Salem tried unflexing one set of claws to free a paw. His weight suddenly shifted, threatening to tear loose the other three. He scrabbled at the plaster with the paw until his claws bit again. "You have me over a barrel," he admitted. "And everything else, for that matter. Ask away, but you have to answer questions for me, too."

"Why should I? You're the one who's hanging up there like a bad lamp."

The smile of an upside-down cat is a sinister thing to see. "Because *you're* the one who'd have to explain things to a bunch of very angry witches when they catch you."

"So, I won't let them catch me."

Salem twitched an ear forward. "Did I just hear an IQ drop? Sabrina caught a magical cold called spellfluenza that caused her to sneeze her powers into you. All she has to do is sneeze again and the powers go back. You go to school together. It's bound to happen sooner or later."

Libby hadn't thought of that. "Rats," she snarled. "You're right. I couldn't transfer away. I've spent my life getting this town to eat out of my hand. It would take forever to break in a new student body at another school."

"You think like a strategist. I like that." Salem's tail twitched in admiration.

"Thanks," Libby responded absently, her brow furrowed as she juggled scenarios in her head. She snapped her fingers. "Sabrina lost her powers to me. You said that you'd lost your powers. That means that magical powers are transferable. So all I've got to do is get someone to give me powers!"

A strange snarfling sound over her head puzzled Libby until she realized that Salem was laughing at her. "Fat chance!" the cat chortled. "Sabrina lost hers to a 24-hour bug, and mine were taken away by the head of the Witches' Council—a power-mad megalomaniac named Drell."

"Why did he take your powers away?"

Salem suddenly found the dust on the molding fascinating. "Umm . . . well, I had this little plan for world conquest that he didn't approve of . . ."

Libby cocked her head. "Climbing up the infrastructure or dominating from the top?"

"Excuse me?"

Libby looked impatient. She waved her hand in a circle. "Conquering the world. How were you going to go about it?"

Salem's favorite topic in the whole world, aside from the dinner menu, was his beloved plan for world domination. And since he'd never really gotten to put it into action to see it work, it had played itself out in countless internal movies. Here was a chance to expound on it, and to a very attentive listener. "Okay, first I was going to . . ."

Quite a while later, Libby sat back in the chair

and pursed her lips. "So this Drell is the all-powerful head of the Witches' Council, and he's the one who took away your powers and condemned you to be a cat."

"For a hundred years," sighed Salem.

Libby got up from the chair and paced thoughtfully back and forth beneath Salem's dangling form. Finally she stopped and threw him a calculating look. "How would you like a chance to regain your powers and get back at Drell at the same time?"

"Sounds interesting," Salem allowed. "How about letting me down to talk about it?"

Libby backed away from the cat, shaking a finger at him. "After we come to an agreement. First, how did Sabrina catch her disease?"

"Spellfluenza is a witch microbe. It floats around or settles into carpets. When it touches a witch who hasn't had it before, it infects them. Afterward, the witch is immune to it."

"Do you know if Drell has ever had spellfluenza?"

Salem's eyebrows shot up. "Heck, no! He's so paranoid about getting sick that he's got a witch doctor on retainer to prevent illnesses." He squinted in thought. "Of course, it's Wednesday, so the witch doctor is out playing golf, and Drell *never* pays him on time. . . ." He looked down at Libby with sudden hope. "Are you thinking what I'm thinking?"

"Are there any of those spellfluenza germs

around here?" Libby spread her hands to indicate Sabrina's room.

"There's probably lots in the carpet," Salem said eagerly. "Use your magic. Just point down and think about a cloud of golden sparkles."

Libby stared at the carpet and made swirling motions with her hands. A puff of golden glitter rose from the fibers of the carpet to form a ball in midair. Libby dumped the pencils out of the small black cauldron that sat on Sabrina's desk and gestured the sparkles into it. Walking over to the closet, she rooted around to find some piece of clothing that was hanging in a dry cleaner's bag. It was a long search. "What— does this girl *wash* everything herself? How *ordinaire.*"

Finally Libby found a black velvet jumper that was enshrouded in a clear, filmy plastic. She ripped off a section, stretched it over the mouth of the cauldron and knotted the rest around the rim. She held the cauldron and its glowing contents up for Salem's inverted inspection. "Here's the plan. You take me to Drell. I use this on him. You get Drell's powers and banish him to wherever you want, leaving you in charge of everything. In exchange, you promise to give me my own magical powers. Deal?"

Salem opened his mouth to speak, then hesitated. What a chance! But the last time he'd plotted against the Witches' Council he'd been caught and punished. He was already a cat—what might they do to him a second time? Turn him into a toilet bowl?

Then again, this was a plan by a truly imaginative despot-to-be. And if it worked, Salem could become a witch again! He could rule over everything! What joy! Salem grinned. "You're a girl after my own heart. Lucky for me I keep it safe in my chest." He carefully worked a paw loose and scratched an "X" in the plaster. "Deal," he said.

Libby gestured and Salem plummeted to the floor, writhing and twisting at the last instant to land heavily on his feet. "Sorry," Libby said with a shrug. "Haven't got the fine-tuning down yet."

Salem executed an elaborate stretch, curving like a Slinky toy as he worked the kinks out of his limbs. "No problem. You should've seen the mess I made the first time I tried levitating food."

"Spew! How rude." Libby snapped her fingers at him. "How do we get to Drell?"

Salem flicked his tail toward the bedroom door. "Straight through the linen closet and hang a right at the towels. It's a shortcut." He trotted forward.

Libby raised her hand to stop him. "One last request before we go."

Salem sat on his haunches and stared coldly at

the cheerleader disguised as Sabrina. There was always a hitch. "And what might that request be?"

Libby looked down at herself, wrinkling her nose in disgust. "How do I get out of this body?"

Salem twitched his tail toward the book. "Page 159."

Chapter 9

☆

Sabrina walked alone down Collins Street, moving as slowly as she could, dreading what her aunts would say when they found out that she had lost her powers. After all, the witch doctor *had* told her to stay home for the twenty-four hours. Sabrina was sure that her aunts wouldn't understand why she couldn't skip school that day. Especially since, with all the worrying and fretting she'd done over her wandering powers, she had completely blown the auditions anyway. Maybe she could slip up to her room unnoticed and pretend to be asleep before they returned.

No such luck. Down the block from her, both Zelda and Hilda Spellman were standing on the front steps, having some kind of altercation with a short, angry-looking man. There was a battered yellow taxi parked at the curb in front of their house, so the little man, who looked to Sabrina like an overstuffed sausage topped by a balding bowling ball, was probably the taxi's driver. As Sabrina drew closer, Zelda pointed at her and said to the driver, "Here comes our niece now, so you *couldn't* have driven her here."

The man wheeled to stare at Sabrina. His eyes bugged out a little and flicked back and forth between her and the house looming behind the aunts. Then his natural orneriness, a survival trait common to all taxi drivers, reared up and fought back. "You *did* sneak out back and try to stiff me! You owe me two-fifty for the trip from the mall, plus five bucks waiting time. *And* my tip."

Zelda looked confused. "Sabrina, did you really take a taxi home?"

"No," said Sabrina automatically. Then a sudden thought struck her. "But I might have. Aunt Zelda, could you pay the man for me so we can discuss this inside?"

Zelda's eyebrows drew together until they met over her nose. "Might have?" she asked with concern. "Is there something going on that we should know about, Sabrina?"

"It's been a cursed day, if you know what I mean, Aunt Zelda." She glanced meaningfully at the taxi driver, who was ogling Hilda at the moment. "I'll pay you back, I promise."

"I'll take care of it," chirped Hilda, taking some crisp new bills from her wallet. She counted out ten singles and handed them to the driver. "Keep the change."

The man made the money disappear as fast as a witch could have and then set his fists on his hips. "Now we can talk about paying for those flats I got when I parked in front of your house," he said belligerently. "The tow truck'll be here any minute and he'll want money, too."

The frown on Zelda's face told Sabrina that the driver was cruising into dangerous territory. "Why should we pay for the way you drive your taxi?"

"Lissen, lady. I've been driving a hack since before I left high school, and that's twenty-one years last July. I ain't never gotten more than one flat on my cab. So if I get two flats in front of your house, it's gotta be someone else's fault, so it gets billed to this little girl's fare."

The driver didn't notice Zelda snap her fingers in annoyance but Sabrina did, so it was less of a surprise to her than to the driver when her aunt suddenly asked in a voice that dripped insincere sweetness, "What flats are you talking about?"

The little man's piggy eyes flashed in exasperation. These women couldn't seem to grasp the obvious. He spun around and pointed at his hack. "Those two flats right . . ." His voice faltered and his jaw dropped.

The taxi sitting at the curb had a faded paint job and a collection of dings and scrapes, but the four tires it rested on were sound and full of air.

The driver's mouth chewed air as confusion settled down upon him. He ran over to his cab to examine the tires more closely. As he did, a tow truck took the corner on two wheels, spun in a loop to present its back end toward the cab, and screeched to a halt. Within seconds the cabbie and the truck driver were hip-deep in a furious argument, with the tow man demanding money for the call, false alarm or not.

Zelda smiled with secret satisfaction as the two men wrestled verbally. She opened the front door of the house and motioned her sister and her niece inside. "That should keep them busy for quite a while. Shall we move on to the subject of why you 'might' have used a taxi if you clearly didn't?"

They all walked into the kitchen and sat down at the table. Sabrina tried to postpone her doom by addressing her younger aunt. "Thank you for paying for the taxi, Aunt Hilda. I'll pay you back by doing extra chores or babysitting or—"

"Oh, don't worry about it. I paid him with Moral Money. They were giving samples of it away at the Hexpo. It's ninety-eight percent temptation-free—you can only spend it on things that aren't fun. It was developed by some witches in the Treasury Bureau, but they found out that politicians couldn't spend it, so they scrapped the test batch and gave it away for use as party favors."

"Stories about financial frivolity can wait, Hilda," Zelda said in a clipped voice. "I think Sabrina has something to tell us that she's avoiding." She turned to face her niece.

Hilda spun on her as well. "Okay, kid, spill it."

Sabrina did her best to hide while in plain sight. "Well, I . . . um . . ."

"Oh, come on, it can't be *that* bad," prompted Zelda.

Sabrina screwed up her face and blurted it all out at once. "I-lost-my-powers-to-Libby-Chessler-and-I-can't-get-them-back-because-I-don't-know-where-she-went-to."

"I was wrong," Zelda said, pressing her hand to her lips. "That's bad."

Hilda hugged her niece around the shoulders. "Sabrina, that's terrible. How did it happen?"

Sabrina fought back tears. "I caught this disease that the witch doctor called 'spellfluenza.' It causes a witch to—"

Zelda held up a hand. "Say no more. We know what it is. We've both had it."

"Yeah," admitted Hilda wryly. "When I had it, I sneezed my powers into Nostradamus. Took me months of hanging around him before I could sneeze them back again. By then he was big on the prediction circuit and thought I was one of his groupies." Her face twisted in distaste. "I got *so* tired of hearing, 'Want me to tell your future, little girl?' "

Zelda took Sabrina's hand in concern. "Why didn't you stay home? It's only a twenty-four-hour bug."

"I should have," admitted Sabrina. "But I really wanted to get into the Thespian Society, and today was auditions but I sneezed my powers into Mr. Pool and Jenny and Harvey and Libby but I didn't get them back from her and she cast a spell that changed the rules."

"Whoa, let's break that down into bite-size chunks," Hilda said. "Libby got your powers and was able to cast a spell with them?"

"Yes!" moaned Sabrina. "And then she left school in a taxi." Sudden realization dawned on her. She whirled to point out the door at the yellow taxi that was tearing away from the curb, swerving around the tow truck and leaving a burnt rubber trail. "That one!"

"Calm down," urged Zelda. "All we have to do is cast a simple spell to find out where Libby is right now, bring her here, and keep her here until you sneeze again." Rising from the table, she used her right hand to trace a large rectangle in midair. "Map!" she commanded, and the rectangle filled with an aerial view of the town of Westbridge. Faint colored lines overlaid the image, providing map coordinates and street names.

"Don'tcha just love it?" Hilda nudged Sabrina. "It's the latest from the A La Chart Map catalog."

Hilda turned to her niece. "We need something connected with our target to do a search. Do you have anything of Libby's?"

"Only her contempt," replied Sabrina.

"That will do," said Zelda. She passed her hand over Sabrina and a shimmering ice-blue cloud shot through with streaks of murky red venom became visible around the teenage girl. Zelda took a pinch of the cloud between her fingers and flung it at the map. The microcloud skittered across the surface of the map, scanning it at unbelievable speed. But it found nothing to stick to, and so fell off the bottom of the map to splatter noiselessly on the floor.

"That's odd," observed Zelda. "Libby isn't anywhere near town. I'll zoom out and try again." A wave of her hands made the scale of the map shrink until the magical rectangle contained a large portion of central New England. Another pinch wrenched from the cloud was thrown at the map to do its high-speed scan. All that resulted was another soundless splat on the floor. "It's like she vanished from the face of the Earth," Zelda said in puzzlement.

Sabrina was staring in disgust at the cloud wrapped around her. "Uh . . . can we get rid of this now, Aunt Zelda?"

"I only made visible what was already there."

"Yeah, but it's easier to take if I don't see it all the time."

Zelda waved her hand in a loop and then

yanked. The cloud paled and then disappeared with a small "foof!"

Suddenly the toaster on the table in front of them quivered, and, like the product of a split-second volcanic eruption, a stiff white folder popped out, landing on the tabletop. It popped open, and a booming voice filled with fury spoke, rattling the windows and shaking the room. "SABRINA SPELLMAN! SEE ME— *ACHOO!*—IMMEDIATELY!"

Sabrina cringed back in her chair. "Oh, no!" she moaned. "Drell knows about it already! He's gonna kill me!"

Hilda stuck out her chin defiantly. "Over our dead bodies! Right, Zelda?"

"I wouldn't put it quite that way, but yes, we'll go with you, Sabrina."

The three witches marched solemnly up the stairs and came to a halt on the landing in front of the linen closet door. Sabrina suddenly turned around and tried to bolt into her room. "I don't want to go! You guys go first and find out what he's gonna do to me!"

Her aunts grabbed her, one arm each, and checked her momentum. "You've got to face him sooner or later," Zelda said.

"Okay, I'll take later."

"No, I wouldn't do that if I were you," said Hilda with a no-nonsense shake of her head. She was the local authority on Drell, since she'd nearly married him centuries before. Drell had stood her up at the altar, though—the Parthenon. "Drell's mad now," Hilda warned, "so he'll do whatever pops into his head. That could be bad, but if you wait, he'll have time to think up something *really* awful."

Sabrina crumpled. "I guess you're right. I've lost my powers to Libby. She'll have me run out of school even if I survive Drell. What can be worse than that?"

There was a sudden rumbling sound, and a brilliant light illuminated the inside of the linen closet. The door burst open and two forms tumbled out, rolling on the carpet like they'd been launched by a spring. The smaller form clawed its way out from under the larger one, leaving bloody furrows.

"Oh, my," said Zelda, her face pale with shock. "It's Salem . . . and Drell!"

Chapter 10

Salem leaped straight up into the air, dodging the long, meaty arm that took a ham-fisted swing at him. "You mangy, flea-bitten future set of violin strings!" Drell roared, lurching to his feet and lunging for Salem, hands outstretched, fingers ready to grab and crush.

"Help!" Salem yowled, and dashed into Sabrina's room.

Drell charged after him, but Zelda waved her hand and set up a glittering force field across the doorway, blocking him.

"Let me through, I have a cat to vivisect!" Drell barked.

"You'll do no such thing!" snapped Zelda primly.

"What's your problem, Drell?" Hilda demanded.

Drell froze as if suddenly realizing what he was doing. He made a great production of relaxing and putting himself in proper order. He sniffed imperiously and, straightening his lavishly frilled powder blue silk shirt, said in a perfectly rational voice, "As head of the Council, I command you to let me through."

"No way!" Sabrina stepped forward, adding her body to the barrier. She had no idea where her courage was coming from. After all, Drell was the kind of guy who turned back-talkers into backflipping Chihuahuas. She braced herself for an instant, then, when nothing happened, thrust out her chin and said, "I don't know what's going on, but you're not going anywhere near Salem!"

"You tell 'im!" came Salem's muffled voice from far inside Sabrina's closet.

Zelda stepped in front of Drell as well. "Will you explain what is going on?"

"It's business," Drell growled, adding with a roar, "None of yours!"

"Council or no Council, you are still in our house and you owe us a civil explanation," Zelda snapped back.

Drell clamped his jaw shut, his lower lip thrust out. He sniffed disdainfully again, but otherwise stood stone-silent.

"You'll never get anything out of him now," Hilda remarked. "He can stay like that for days. But I know someone we can get to talk." She snapped her fingers at Sabrina's room. Salem came floating out, an unseen hand carrying him by the scruff of the neck.

"Hey," he complained. "If I was supposed to fly, I'd have my own private plane."

Salem floated to a halt in front of Zelda. "Salem, why were you in the Other Realm?"

Salem opened his mouth to speak, but Drell shot him a thunderous look. The cat shut his mouth without speaking.

"Salem, *what is going on?*" Zelda demanded.

Drell pushed forward and clapped an arm around Zelda's shoulders. He smiled down at her. "Nothing is going on," he said, oozing false cheeriness. "Is it?" he added significantly to Salem.

Salem forced a grin. "Nope, heh-heh. Nothing happening here, except maybe the imminent demise of an innocent house pet . . ."

Hilda had had enough. She cocked her finger like a gun and put it to Salem's head. "You have five seconds, furball."

"It wasn't my fault, honest!" Salem blurted, shrinking back. "Libby double-crossed me!"

A vast rumbling filled the hallway as Drell darkened, brewing up a thunderstorm of fury. He flung his arms at Salem, as if hurling a great ball of magic.

Nothing happened.

And then Drell sneezed. Salem looked at him

with unashamed relief. "I forgot. You're firing blanks now." He grinned at Hilda. "He can't hurt me. Can you put me down now?" Stunned, Hilda pointed her finger and Salem dropped down onto the wicker hamper at the corner of the stairwell.

The three female witches turned slowly to stare at the huge male witch. Hilda broke the silence. "Is it true, Drell?"

Drell, stubbornly silent again, turned beet-red and stared daggers at the cat. Then he sneezed four times in rapid succession, finishing with a long, disgusting snort that sounded like a garbage disposal trying to grind backward.

"Yup," said Salem, licking the tip of his tail but keeping a wary eye on Drell. "No powers. Lost 'em to a teenage girl, no less."

Drell's body shook with suppressed rage as he glared at Salem. "Changing you into a cat was too good for you! I should have turned you into a fondue set—*ACHOO!*"

"Should have thought of that when you were still the Omnipotent Overlord," Salem purred.

Hilda snapped her fingers and the invisible hand jerked Salem up by the scruff again. "No more games, cat! Out with the story!"

Hanging helplessly in midair, Salem sighed. "Libby promised to get me my powers back if I took her to Drell, but before she opened the cauldron she banished me back to the closet."

"Cauldron?" said Sabrina. "What cauldron?"

"The cauldron from your desk with the spellfluenza germs in it."

Zelda blanched. "You don't mean she took spellfluenza germs to Drell . . . ?"

"And infected him?" finished Hilda.

"When Drell sneezed, 'poof'!" Salem finished, and, as if to punctuate the remark, Drell sneezed again, this time so violently he almost knocked himself off his feet. When he wiped his nose on his sleeve, Sabrina turned away, totally grossed-out. When she glanced back, he was still standing by Hilda, his hands clenched, his head turned away but held high, chin outthrust—the very portrait of a tortured but determined survivor.

Hilda placed her small hand over his massive one and said softly, "Don't worry, Drell. Powers or no powers, I'll stand by you."

"A magnanimous offer, considering I'm powerless to stop you," he answered just as softly, but with a sarcastic bite to it. He raised one hand gracefully—then slammed it into his forehead and sobbed, throwing himself on Hilda. "Oh, Hilda, Hilda, Hilda! What am I going to do?" he cried, his great body quivering as he blubbered like a baby.

Hilda summoned all her strength and barely managed to push Drell back. "You can start by letting *go* of me and training your meat hooks to behave!"

Drell seemed to shrink into himself. He gazed out at her with big, moist eyes. "But I'm *so* despondent. I need comforting."

"You need therapy," retorted Hilda.

Sabrina zapped a small floral box into her hand. "He needs a tissue."

"Sabrina!" Zelda said. "You have your powers back!"

Sabrina was so surprised she dropped the tissues. "Ohmigosh, you're right!" She held up her index fingers and smiled at them as if they were made of gold, realizing only now just how much she'd missed her magic. "I'm a witch again!"

"I'm celebrating already," muttered Drell, bending down and snatching up the fallen tissue box. Plucking one out, he blew his nose, honking like a foghorn in a misty harbor.

"Of course!" Zelda mused. "When Drell sneezed, his powers fled to the nearest nonwitch."

"And since his powers are so much stronger than Sabrina's, they knocked *her* powers out of Libby and back into Sabrina!" said Hilda.

"Totally bypassing me," Salem growled. "Nobody ever thinks of the cat."

"Wow, Libby achieved Ultimate Power faster than even she'd have thought," Sabrina observed. "There's a scary image."

"And a dangerous one," said Zelda. "Which is why we've got to convince her to give up those powers."

"Libby? Willingly give up the power to satisfy her every whim, before she even whimsies it?" Sabrina shook her head. "Not likely."

"I'll convince her," Drell said in a low, evil tone. "Just lemme at her. I'll get my powers back if I have to unravel her like a frayed han . . . hhhan . . ." His nose twitched desperately. ". . . KIE!" came the sneeze, and Drell dropped the tissue box. "I hate this!" he yelled, stamping his feet in pure rage.

Hilda smiled condescendingly at her big ex-boyfriend. "Drell. Please. She'd turn you into a toadstool before you got within ten feet of her. She's one of the most powerful witches in existence now, remember?"

"Oh, rub it in, why don't you!" Drell picked up the tissue box again and repeated the foghorn, looking pathetically despondent. For the first time in her witch life, Sabrina felt sorry for him.

"So what do we do?" she asked. "I mean, Drell's powers now reside in a spoiled cheerleader with delusions of global control. I can't think of anything more terrifying."

Hilda turned to face the linen closet, her face set in an expression of dubious determination. "We do whatever we can do, I suppose."

"Yes," Zelda said apprehensively. "If worldwide witchery were to be controlled by a mortal, it could cause damage of unimaginable proportions throughout the natural and supernatural realms."

"Not to mention the witches whose cover she could blow, including our own," Sabrina added. The thought of being called "freak" at school made her stomach turn. It was bad enough when Libby called her that. If everyone did . . . if *Harvey* did . . . she'd simply die.

Hilda grimaced. "Yeah. I don't think the world is ready for the truth about Michael Jackson, Roseanne, and Bill Gates."

Sabrina turned to her aunt. "Bill Gates is a witch?"

Hilda put on her "Are you kidding?" face. "How do you think he became the Nine-Billion-Dollar Nerd?"

"You didn't think Windows Ninety-five sold because it was original, did you?" added Zelda. "Magical reverse-engineering is very big in Silicon Valley."

"Ladies—" Drell interrupted.

"Watch it, blubbo!" shot Salem. Drell's powerlessness was making him dangerously cocky.

"Okay, ladies and future *cheese pot,*" Drell said, bowing to Salem, "can we cut the dish and go rescue the universe while there's still one to save?"

Sabrina nodded agreement, even though the mere thought of facing Libby Chessler pumped up with Drell's powers was almost enough to paralyze her. "Let's go."

Everyone nodded, and Sabrina grasped the handle to the linen closet and swung the door open. They filed in one by one, with Sabrina going in last. As she shut the door she thought, *After this, Stephen King books will never scare me again.*

Chapter 11

Once the linen closet door was closed, the flash of light and its accompanying thunder were the same as usual, as was the sense of being turned inside out as Sabrina, her aunts, Salem, and Drell traveled through *somewhere* to bypass ten million light-years of real distance. But the *there* when they got *there* was completely different. And while the Spellman witches (and their cat) were merely shocked, Drell was horrified. "My Magritte decor is gone! Where's my apple? Where are my vines? Where are my parsecs of beautiful blue *nothing?*"

As head of the Witches' Council, Drell's taste controlled the very appearance of the Other Realm. Over the centuries he had varied the look of the place according to his changing whims. His most recent motif had been taken from the

Surrealist school of paintings. Everything had floated in an endless sky-blue space flecked with fluffy clouds. Living, moving vines and trailers provided leafy carpets to walk on and furniture to sit on. Fish draped in pearl necklaces swam through the air around a weightless marble pillar topped with an enormous green apple.

When you have witch-power, it's easy to decorate with the impossible.

But now, none of that remained. Instead, the five witches found themselves in a green marble and crystal atrium leading to a two-story-high pair of glass doors. Flanking the doors were wide display windows with top fashion designs worn casually by six identical mannequins. The face appearing in dozens of artfully placed chrome-framed ads along the bottom of the windows was the same face as those of the mannequins, one kissing a lipstick, another snuggling up to cans of hairspray, and numberless others beaming proud ownership of various other glittering consumer goodies. Emblazoned on every product, on every shop tag, and etched in ornate script on the glass doors twenty feet high were the letters "LC."

"What has she done to my realm?" wailed Drell. Sabrina was sure he was about to say something more, but four sneezes in a row cut him off.

"Oh, this is ridiculous," Hilda said, and with a

quick point she magicked something into the palm of her hand.

"Is that a little ice cube?" asked Sabrina curiously.

"No, it just looks like one," Hilda said, and she held it out for Drell. "Take it. It can't cure you, but it'll plug the pipes for a while."

Clearly Drell resented accepting Hilda's help, but he didn't want to keep sneezing either. He took the pill and swallowed it, but immediately grasped his throat. "It's cold!"

Hilda shrugged. "Of course. It's a cold pill."

As Sabrina watched in fascination, Drell's nose slowly turned blue. Frost formed over it, and a single little white icicle grew down from the tip. Drell crossed his eyes and gawked at it. "By doze! You froze by doze!"

Hilda sighed. "Look, do you want to stop sneezing or don't you?"

With supreme effort, Drell reined in a tirade. After all, he wasn't sneezing now, as promised. "Alride, alride, led's juzz ged odd wid it."

They examined their surroundings more closely. "So," Zelda said, "Libby has turned the Other Realm into a shopping mall."

"And starring her favorite person," said Sabrina, pointing at the mannequins and the ads. "Everything has Libby's face on it."

Salem pawed at the brickwork underfoot. A spiral of golden bricks spun out from a spot in the middle of the atrium and, after making several widening turns around itself, straightened out and made a beeline for the great glass doors. "This is architectural design?" Salem sniffed.

"By way of MGM, I think," said Sabrina, studying the green fluted towers and the yellow brick path leading into the mall. "It looks like this is supposed to be the Emerald City of Oz."

"It doesn't look a thing like it," objected Zelda critically.

"Deither did the boovie," snapped Drell. "Dow, are we goind doo stad here ad debate the woefully idadequade cultural depth of a pubescend rah-rah queed, or are we goind to do sobethind aboud gedding by bowers back?" He heaved his bulk forward, stomping angrily toward the glass doors, his frozen nose leaving a wispy frost trail behind him. Sabrina's aunts reluctantly followed, but Sabrina, noticing that Salem wasn't with them, looked behind her for the cat.

Salem sat in the middle of the gold-brick spiral, watching them leave. He, of all of them, most feared the dangers of going up against the powers that Libby now commanded. After all, he had gone up against them when they were Drell's, and he'd lost. Whatever this mall-world had in store for them, he knew it would be something they'd never expect.

"Salem?" Sabrina prompted.

The cat hesitated. "Oh, all right, I'm coming." He hauled himself to his feet, complaining, "But the first person who calls me 'Toto' gets bitten."

As they neared the towering glass doors they spied a uniformed doorman standing at a lectern that blocked any further access. He was a short, tubby man with a head like a bowling ball. Something about him struck Sabrina as familiar. He stepped forward and held up his hand to halt them. "Whaddaya gonna buy?" he demanded.

That voice—it was the driver from the taxi that Libby had taken to Sabrina's house! *I guess Libby believes in recycling after all,* she thought.

Drell bristled at the obstruction. "We're nod cobing to buy anyding!"

The doorman rotated his chin forward. "Can't come in, then. This is a shopping mall. It sells stuff."

Zelda tried to clarify their situation for the doorman. "We're here to see Libby," she told him earnestly.

"Oh, that's different," said the doorman, bustling back to his lectern and picking up a clipboard. He looked up at the group. "You major-name fashion designers?" he asked, tapping a line on the clipboard with a pencil.

"No," Zelda replied, slightly puzzled.

"Hotshot Hollywood producers?"

"No."

"Worshipful admirers hoping to get a glimpse of the Consumer Goddess?"

"Of course n—" Zelda began angrily.

"Yes!" interrupted Sabrina, jumping between her aunt and the doorman. "We're her biggest fans and we'd love to get to meet her in person!"

The doorman squinted at his clipboard. "Sorry, The Libby's groupie list is already filled for the next ten years. I can add ya, though."

"*'The'* Libby? Isn't that a mite egocentric?" whispered Zelda to her sister.

"Comes with the job," Hilda whispered back, jerking her head toward the glowering Drell.

Sabrina continued her plea. "But we need to see her now."

"Nobody sees The Libby," said the doorman firmly. "Not nobody, not nohow."

Salem took a break from grooming his whiskers to ask, "If we bought something, could we get in to see her?"

"Depends on whatcha bought," replied the doorman, changing clipboards. He consulted a fee schedule. "Simple purchase will getcha in, of course. But in order to see The Libby, ya'd hafta spend enough to catch her interest. She loves competitive shopping."

Drell took out his wallet, opening it to allow a cascade of charge cards in a plastic holder to tumble toward the floor. "Okay, whad will it take doo get 'De' Libby's attention?" he asked in a voice that dripped sarcasm as obvious as the icicle on his nose. "I've got the Despot's Card, Sorcerer's Club, Aberican Hexpress . . ."

The doorman's hand went up again. "Sorry, the mall only accepts cash or the LibbyCard. And ya'd have to spend . . ." He pressed a button to light up an LED display. ". . . six million, three hunnerd thousand bucks."

"Whad?" Drell's stuffy-nosed outrage was deafening.

"That's how much she's spent so far," the doorman explained. "As of an hour ago, that is. You'd have to match that just to get her to know you're here."

Drell swelled to his full height and his cheeks turned red. He was getting so hot with anger that his nose started to thaw. Just as the little icicle melted off, Hilda quickly darted between him and the doorman and produced a handful of currency. "What will five dollars buy us?"

The doorman snickered. "In this place? Nothing!" His snicker erupted into full-scale laughter that grew until tears ran down his face and he had to gasp for breath.

Drell moved forward to pummel the doorman into an ugly little grease spot when the sound of two metal "pings" chimed through the air. Iron boots appeared out of nowhere and clamped onto his feet. Suddenly rooted in place, Drell's upper body jerked forward, and he had to flap his arms in wild circles to regain his balance.

Automatically the giant witch turned on

Hilda, who still had her finger pointed at his feet. She met his eyes and raised the finger to shake "no" at him. Drell snarled, baring his teeth in an impressive display of animal aggression, but he finally subsided with smoldering acceptance.

The doorman, who had been giggling all this time, wiped his eyes and struggled to stand upright. "Hoo-boy, I ain't laughed like that inna dog's age! Tell ya what—just for that, I'm gonna bend a rule." He dug a crumpled rectangle of cardboard out of his jacket pocket. "I'll sell ya this LibbyLotto ticket for five bucks. That'll at least get ya into the mall. From there on, though, you're on your own. Hee-hee!" Chuckling all over again, the doorman hit a switch and the great glass doors swung majestically open. Zelda released Drell's feet from their restraints and they all entered the mall.

It was breathtaking. Sabrina stopped in her tracks and just stared, noticing from the corner of her eye that her companions were doing the same thing.

The interior of the mall might have been designed by the famous Dutch engraver, M.C. Escher. It was an enormous space filled with crisscrossing walkways, some of them right-side-up, others facing sideways and even upside-down. Gravity only existed in relation to the walkways, keeping a shopper at right angles to that particular "floor" at that moment. But that was the only definition of "down" in the gargantuan shopping center.

Seeming to be constructed out of layers and layers of balconies and catwalks, every direction that Sabrina looked resembled a view down an enormous stairwell lined with glittering storefronts. The only rule seemed to be that each store had a stretch of walkway in front of it. The walkways themselves were completely unrestrained, winding around and through shops, cutting through other catwalks, or leaping across great voids to reach lone shops hanging "upside-down" in space.

Everywhere Sabrina looked, bustling, faceless consumers milled about, their arms filled with packages and shopping bags. Depending on what path they were on, they walked upside-down or at bizarre sharp angles to other people on paths a few feet above or below them. Walks that were adjacent originated from different levels and allowed no crossing over between them. Two stores a mere ten feet from each other could be miles apart via the twisting paths.

The most amazing thing of all was that the mall had no boundaries. As far as Sabrina could tell, it went on forever in all directions. A shopper without a guide would get hopelessly lost in this maze within minutes, and once lost, they'd be stuck there forever. Sabrina figured that was the point.

"How are we going to find Libby in all of this?" Hilda moaned.

"Salem," said Sabrina, "can you follow her trail with your nose?"

Salem's ears flattened against his skull. "I don't do dog's work."

"Whoa, sorry I asked." Sabrina indicated the yellow brick road. "I guess we should follow this then."

"Lead on," urged Zelda.

Sabrina started forward, following the yellow brick road up a gentle rise, and when she reached the top, a whole new amazing sight met her eyes. Below, at the end of the yellow brick road, was a huge—a gargantuan—spherical object hovering above a pedestal. "It looks like a model of a small moon," Zelda observed. "Why would they have that here?"

Salem's eyes widened. "That's no moon— that's the shopping mall!"

Amazed, the group hurried over to the object, which Sabrina could now determine was some twenty feet high and therefore twenty feet in diameter. And inside was a perfect model of the mall, down to every last detail.

In the center was a tiny replica of the towering glass doors they'd just gone through, reduced now to the size of rice kernels. Millimeters beyond it a little red dot winked brightly and a little holographic label flashed "YOU ARE LOST HERE." If Sabrina squinted she could see a tiny globe—a model of this model—at the base of the winking dot. "Too weird," she murmured.

Then she noticed the sign to her right that read "PUSH BUTTON FOR SERVICE." "Here goes nothing," she told the group, and jabbed her thumb down on it.

A panel in the platform slid aside and a desk rose up from the floor. Seated behind the desk was an elfin man in a dark suit and a rather dated bowler hat. He smiled impishly at the crowd before him.

"Skippy!" boomed Drell. His nose had almost completely thawed by now, so his pronunciation was back to normal. "What are you doing here?"

Skippy, the Overlord's official Underling, never spoke aloud. With an apologetic grin he gestured at his feet. Sabrina leaned over the desk and saw that he was attached to the desk with a ball and chain.

"Bum rap," Drell said with no sympathy in his voice whatsoever. "Look, Skippy, what can you do about helping us solve our little problem here?"

Skippy's face fell and he shook his head sadly. He held his hands up together and a coil of hempen rope popped into existence and wrapped around his wrists.

"Your hands are tied, huh?" Drell noted.

Skippy nodded, and the ropes "poofed" away.

"So Libby doesn't just control this realm, she controls you, too?" Zelda asked.

A TV remote control appeared in front of Skippy and clicked loudly. Like a switched-off video picture, Skippy's form broke into lines and then dissolved into fleeing colored dots. A second later, he was back again, whole.

"She threatened to atomize you?" Sabrina said, shocked.

"Now that's an effective management technique," Hilda quipped.

Now Skippy's head morphed into Libby's face and then into an angry lap dog's, silently yapping and snapping the air.

"I know what you mean," said Sabrina. "I have to put up with her every day at school."

"But is there anything you can do to help us?" Zelda asked him.

Skippy's face squinched up in a thoughtful expression, and then he beamed a huge smile and snapped his fingers. Making an elaborate production of looking carefully around him, peering up and down for good measure and somehow assuring himself that Libby wasn't watching, he made a magical flourish with both hands. A brightly printed window card appeared between his palms. It read, "PLAY LIBBY-LOTTO! WIN BIG! *First Prize—anything you desire in the mall!*"

Another gesture and an electronic terminal materialized on the desktop. Witch-light lettering glowed "LIBBYLOTTO!" above the monitor. Running lights streamed along the edges of the box, converging on a slot intended for inserting tickets.

Hilda snorted. "That's it? Play her silly game and hope we win?"

The TV remote control reappeared, floating a few inches away from a globe of the Earth. It clicked, and small replicas of Libby's mall began to dot the planet's surface. The dots thickened until no spot on the globe remained free of them.

"Great," said Drell. "Going up against her isn't enough of a gamble—we have to gamble just to get *at* her first!"

"Okay, so that's our only choice," said Sabrina. "But what are our odds of winning?"

A tote board materialized above the terminal and a stream of numbers slid across its face.

"1.4275×10^8 to 1," Sabrina made out. "A little over one chance in ten? That's not too bad."

Zelda looked pityingly at her niece. "Sweetheart, that's times ten to the eighth power," she said gently. "That's about one hundred fifty *million* to one."

Sabrina's hopeful smile wilted. "Oh."

"Ahem," coughed Salem loudly. Everybody turned to look at him. "You people are too honest for your own good. If someone would loan me a smidgen of power, *I'll* show you how it's done."

"You can borrow mine," grumped Drell. "They seem to be very popular at the moment."

"I'll do it," said Hilda, ignoring Drell. "But you're going outside for the next month so I don't have to clean the litter box."

Salem grimaced. "Even if it snows?"

"Might I remind you who is responsible for this little mix-up?"

"Oh, all right, just give me the ticket," Salem said. Sabrina handed him the crumpled cardboard, which he took in his mouth.

Hilda snapped her fingers and a ball of multicolored energy flashed from her into Salem. The cat closed his eyes and said something indistinct around the mouthful of ticket. Suddenly, the tote board above the monitor changed to read, "1 to 1."

"Good going, Salem!" crowed Sabrina, taking the somewhat soggy ticket out of his mouth. "That's a handy spell."

"It was step three in my Master Plan. I would have won every jackpot there was for about twelve hours," he smirked. Then a painful realization set in and his face fell. "But it was a one-shot spell. I can never use it again."

"Well, if it helps us out, it'll be worth it," soothed Sabrina, scratching him behind the ears.

Salem melted under the caress. He lifted his chin so she could scratch under there as well. "I guess you're right," he sighed. "They don't let cats win prizes anyway, do they?"

Sabrina gave him a last slow scratch, then put

the ticket into the slot. "Cross your fingers," she told everybody. The terminal whirred.

The air filled with trumpets, and lights flashed throughout the mall. A thunderous voice echoed through the vast spaces, "WE HAVE A GRAND PRIZE WINNER!"

The monitor on the prize machine sparkled with brilliant flashes and a forty-foot video screen descended from above. Libby's face, three stories tall, filled the screen, cooing, "Congratulations! You have won the LibbyLotto Grand Prize! Through the generosity and ultimate coolness of Libby Chessler, you may have your heart's desire—any one thing in Chessler Mall is yours!"

Sabrina gathered all of her courage up and faced the enormous projected face. "Thank you, Libby. We'll take *you.*"

Chapter 12

Libby's projected face, immaculately modeled with the most expensive makeup, creased into a mask of shock and fury. "What are *you* doing here? I thought I made this place pricey enough that freaks like you couldn't afford to get in!"

Hilda smiled her most sarcastic smile up at the monitor. "We could afford to buy a LibbyLotto ticket from the doorman."

Libby grew so furious that her towering display spun in place several times before coming to rest again. "Oohh, he is like, *so* unemployed!"

Sabrina reissued her challenge. "So, where do we meet you?"

Libby stamped her foot in anger. Sabrina had no idea where her foe physically was at the moment, but the entire mall structure shook with that petulant stamping. The floor beneath

Sabrina and her companions quaked, nearly throwing Zelda off-balance. "You can't!" thundered Libby. "You'll just try and take away my powers! I declare the contest over! Nobody wins!"

"Sorry, luv, you can't do that," interrupted a lilting British accent.

The great monitor pivoted to address the new voice, which belonged to a petite woman in Elizabethan garb and a cute pageboy bob now standing near Skippy at the Information Booth. "Who are you to tell me what to do?" demanded Libby. "I control everything here."

"I'm the Rules Bearer," retorted the woman, straightening her floppy tam and producing a thick scroll. With a flick of her wrist, the scroll flew into the air and with a whirr unrolled to a specific place on the parchment. She read from the document. "Rule 372 states: The Rules Apply To Everyone. I'm afraid it even includes such rarities as yourself."

Libby was reduced to inarticulate frustration. "Arrgh!" she roared.

"I've felt that way many a time myself," Drell said in sympathy.

A whirr and the scroll stopped at another entry. "Rule 195, which is the rule that brought me here, states: Any Object Created By Magic Shall Bear Its Creator's Mark And Be Binding Upon Said Creator." The Rules Bearer looked knowingly up at the monitor.

Libby avoided her gaze. "What's that got to do with me?" she said, brushing imaginary lint off her Donna Karan beaded jacket.

"Your magic made the ticket, luv. *They* won your contest, so *you* have to grant them their prize."

"And if I don't?"

Whirring again. "Rule 909: If A Witch Violates Rule 195, That Witch Shall Be Transformed Into A Dustpan For A Term Not To Exceed Six Hundred Years. Fancy any brooms in particular, ducks?"

"Daddy always says there's a way around any rule," Libby remarked, pondering. Then her eyes lit up and the monitor swiveled to face the Rules Bearer again. "Can I set conditions on them?"

"Oh, my word, yes!" she replied. "Conditions are what rules are all about."

"Then the freak can come see me after she brings me a . . ." Libby squinched her eyes shut, the effort of thinking written on her face. ". . : a torch from the center of the sun!"

"Unfair!" shouted Sabrina. "That's impossible!"

"Imaginative but disallowed," chirped the Rules Bearer. "Rule 721: Trials Shall Be Limited To Not More Than Three In Number And Shall Be Conceivably Winnable By The Contestants."

Libby lost her temper and the mall shook like a giant steel-stamping mill. "What good is being a witch if you can't win all the time?" Her image pointed at Skippy and three wickedly sharp tiny paper airplanes shot out of the monitor and buried themselves nose-deep into the dark mahogany of the desktop, *shh-thunk, shh-thunk, shh-thunk.* "There! Three contests," Libby snarled. Noxious purple clouds billowed out from the screen of the monitor as it snapped upward, vanishing from sight.

"Aren't you going to wish us luck?" Salem called after her.

"I'll give her points for—*ACHOO!*" Drell snuffled. "Showmanship," he finished.

Sabrina and her aunts pried the folded paper darts out of Skippy's desk, smoothing them out to read their challenges. "'Contest Number One,'" read Sabrina. "'Go to the Svelte Pelt and find the coolest clothes.'"

"The second is a riddle to solve," said Zelda. "It reads:

'Fancy wax and carmine dye,
In a storage box am I.
Standard gear for female mortal
Will provide an exit portal.'"

"We have to go to the Storage Store for that one."

"The last one sounds really creepy," said Hilda, curling her lip in distaste. "It says, 'Prepare for the Ultimate Challenge.'"

"I know that we have to save the world from

Libby, but this is beginning to look impossible," said Sabrina. She waved at the huge model of the moon-sized mall. "How are we even supposed to *find* the stores to start?"

"I suppose it's not a violation of the rules for me to state the obvious," the Rules Bearer said, rolling up her scroll. "You *are* at an Information Booth, after all."

Sabrina and her aunts turned to stare at Skippy with wide, hopeful eyes. "Skippy," Sabrina asked. "Can you show us how to get to these stores?"

Skippy stared pointedly at the place where the tall monitor had hung and briefly transformed his head into a yapping dog's again. He extended his hand, palm down. When he turned it over, it held an old-fashioned clicker—a shell of tin with a stiff tongue of spring steel attached to the bottom edge. On the curved surface of the tin was a faded illustration of a pair of ruby slippers, done in paint and chipped enamel. He pressed the metal tongue three times—"clicka, clicka, clicka!" As he clicked, three different locations in the model mall lit up briefly. Then, with a flourish, he tossed the clicker to Sabrina.

"Ooh, goodie, a click-tripper," said Hilda. "All we have to do is click it three times and it'll take us directly to each store. Skippy, I could kiss you!"

Skippy blushed from his scalp to his starched collar and Sabrina noticed the Rules Bearer tense up a little. *I guess there's no rule against interdepartmental crushes here,* thought Sabrina. Then she remembered Libby the Control Queen. *Not yet, anyway.*

Sabrina scooped Salem up in her arms as the others closed in around her. She took a deep breath and pressed the clicker. Clicka, clicka, clicka!

An instant later, all five found themselves standing in a brightly lit store. Everywhere around them were furs and skins of all descriptions. Shaggy buffalo hides were tacked to brightly enameled walls next to black-and-white-striped zebra hides. Nine feet of blinding white polar bear fur, complete with all four paws, clung to the wall by massive claws, while a ring of dingo hides snapped at its flanks. A broad shoulder-level band of tanned anaconda skins circled the store, mouths-to-tails.

The store itself was a furrier's dream. There were racks upon racks of jackets and coats assembled from every kind of animal fur possible. Mink jackets rubbed elbows with 1920-style raccoon coats, leopard stoles slunk at the foot of a royal coronation robe tipped with ermine and seal. One whole corner was a bin of caps, babushkas, mukluks, and even a Beefeater shako.

The tanned goods display brought no shame on the furs. Rows of wallets stood to attention before a reviewing committee of leather belts, ties, and vests, representing the vast array of wearable flesh. Over it all arched a tooled-leather banner proclaiming "The Svelte Pelt."

Salem stared around him in horror. "I've got a feeling I don't want to be here," he muttered.

"Oh, what a lovely Burmese cat," a cheery voice said. "Have you come to have him made into a muff?"

Sabrina whirled to face the speaker. It was Jenny, but a Jenny that Sabrina could never in her life have imagined.

This Jenny's tight red curls were bound back into a severe bun pinned with genuine tortoise-shell combs. Under a sable bolero jacket edged in black suede she wore a chamois shirt above a slinky patent leather skirt. The skirt was bound with a snakeskin belt in the familiar pattern of the American diamondback rattler. Her legs were shaved and firmly booted in loose-topped alligator skin cowboy boots. A rawhide button branded with the words "SAVE THE WAIFS" hung from a lanyard around her neck. Tiny lizard claws dangled from multiple piercings in her ears to complete the outfit. She smiled brightly. "If a muff is too old-fashioned for you, would you consider just having him stuffed and mounted? He'd be just as sleek but have a much lower maintenance."

"Can you take an order for a tea cozy?" asked Drell with a wicked glance at Salem.

"Nobody's making a cozy out of our cat!"

Sabrina said as Salem huddled fearfully behind her legs where he'd darted.

"But he'd make such a stylish addition to any decor," bubbled Jenny. "And anyway, it's just in keeping with the natural order of things."

"It's the natural order to turn animals into decorations?" Sabrina asked, shocked.

"Well, they are beautiful."

"That's an accidental byproduct of natural selection, dear," broke in Zelda. With a long history of scientific research and friends at almost every university in the world, Sabrina's older aunt knew as much about science as she did about magic.

"This is about natural selection, too," Jenny said earnestly. "As the top of the fashion chain, it's our duty to select the best things in the animal world to wear. Animals should be proud that the millions of years they spent growing fur or scales or whatever aren't wasted in jungles and yucky swamps. It's their contribution to confirming our status as the most sophisticated and tasteful species on the planet."

Stepping right up to Jenny, Sabrina peered into her friend's eyes, as if searching for something. "Jenny, is that really you?"

Jenny's fingers snapped in sudden inspiration. "I know! What you need is to check out how superior it makes you feel." She hurried over to a nearby mannequin—that looked like Libby, of course—decked out in a luxurious white fur coat with black stripes. "Siberian tiger fur," Jenny said, removing the coat from the mannequin and bringing it over to Sabrina. "Just try it on. With this on your shoulders you could be the talk of the town!"

"I don't doubt it." Sabrina refused to take the coat and instead turned to her older aunt. "Aunt Zelda, this is awful. Libby's turned Jenny into everything Jenny hates."

Zelda held one hand out, palm up, and with her other hand pointed at it. A little cloth pouch appeared in her palm, artistically embroidered and closed by a pullstring. Zelda opened the pouch, took out a pinch of dust, and tossed it at Jenny. The dust sparkled in a rainbow of color, then settled to a bright red before slowly fading away. "Don't worry, this isn't the Jenny you know," Zelda concluded. "It's a copy of her, as imagined by Libby. She's just doing this to annoy you."

"It's creepy!" said Sabrina, staring at the leather-clad fashion plate. "The real Jenny is so anticruelty that she apologizes to tofu before she eats it."

"I don't care if she eats Bambi in Thumper sauce," interrupted Drell. "We're supposed to be getting my powers back."

"So remember who's helping whom," Hilda warned him. "Or maybe a reprocessed copy of you would be an improvement."

"How dare you—" The words cut off sharply

as Hilda waggled an index finger. Drell shifted his expression to what he thought was regretful romanticism. "The Hilda I used to date would never do that to me," he said softly.

"No, but the Hilda you used to stand up all the time would," snarled Hilda with uncharacteristic annoyance. "Now behave."

"So," broke in Jenny, "would you like to try on the tiger?"

"Uh . . . it's a little exotic for high-school wear," answered Sabrina. "Libby wants us to find the coolest clothes. Can you show us where they are?"

"You'll have to use the changing room," Jenny said. "You can find anything you want in there."

Hilda didn't look impressed. "I've heard of off-the-rack selections, but I don't think I want to try on things off-the-floor."

"I am *not* trying on anything in this store," Salem announced firmly. "And vice versa."

"But I'm sure you'll find what you want in here," Jenny assured them, opening the door to the changing room.

The group entered and found themselves in a hall of mirrors. Big ones, small ones, short ones, tall ones, everywhere they looked were mirrors. It was impossible to tell the room's true dimensions. For all Sabrina knew, this space was really the size of a dressing room. Then again, it might be miles long.

"I've got a bad feeling about this," Salem said.

"Let's see if we can do this some other way," agreed Zelda. The group backtracked and reentered the store to find Jenny dressing a Libby-mannequin in an evening gown made of beautiful white iridescent fur. A long twisting horn hung from a silver chain around its neck. "It's the latest in unicorn chamois," Jenny told them brightly. "It's a one-of-a-kind. Did you find what you were looking for?"

"No, we're done shopping, thanks," said Sabrina, and headed for the door. She received a rude shock when the door remained closed and she banged her nose against the glass.

"I guess that's a hint that we've got to go through the changing room," observed Salem.

"House of mirrors, here we come," said Sabrina without enthusiasm. "Let's go."

They walked through the changing room door into the hall of mirrors as Jenny perkily waved good-bye. The moment they were all in, the door vanished.

Then the lights went out.

Chapter 13

☆

"Now this is challenging," drawled Salem's voice in the darkness.

Hilda's voice chimed in, "I've heard of keeping your opponents in the dark, but this is ridiculous."

The lights came back on, dimly at first, and then they rose to a level that allowed the witches to see themselves in all the mirrors, though enough shadows remained to keep their orientation confused.

Not that the mirrors didn't do that sufficiently on their own. Sabrina stared at herself in the mirror to the left—her reflection stared back, but it was dressed in dungarees and a red checked Pendleton shirt, and it wore a straw hat and had bare feet. The mirror on her right reflected her image dressed in a nurse's uniform. "What kind of mirrors are these?"

Hilda was ogling herself in another mirror. Her reflection was dressed in a space suit. "Fashion Finders from the Good-Looking Glass Company, I'd say," she answered.

"That's exactly what they are," Zelda said, looking at her reflection in yet another mirror. "Rather than ruining a lot of clothes trying them on, witches use these to see how they'd look in an outfit before they buy it." She turned to look at the back of the white silk evening gown and diamond tiara that her reflection was wearing.

"Isn't this divine," Salem remarked, preening in front of a glass that showed him as the Egyptian cat deity Bast.

Drell took one look at himself in the nearest mirror, flinched, and moved away. "Okay, let's get going already." He crossed behind Hilda, pausing long enough to see how they looked together in futuristic unisex jumpsuits. "How very Jetsons." Barely catching a sneeze in a tissue, he passed Sabrina, avoiding his reflection in tattered hillbilly rags. The Armani mirror drew him like a magnet.

"And just where are you going?" Hilda said, an edge in her voice. "Drell, we don't even know how this room operates yet. Don't go wandering off."

Drell stretched up on tiptoe to peer over the tops of the mirrors. "There's no place to wander to," he snapped. "This mirror maze fills the entire room and there are no doors." He folded his arms and leaned back into the corner where two mirrors met, flanked by Drells in a Roman toga and in 1960s hippie garb, complete with patched bellbottoms, tie-dyed T-shirt, and flowers in his hair. "There's no way out."

"No," Sabrina reminded him, "Libby's clue says we have to find the coolest clothes. I think that means we have to look at ourselves in all these mirrors until we find the coolest outfits."

"For all of us, or just one of us?" Hilda asked. "And do we all have to look cool in the same mirror, or do each of us have to find a different mirror?"

Sabrina shrugged. "I guess we should start checking out mirrors."

"The right mirror will *be* the way out," Zelda told her. "At least, let's hope so."

"I think we should split up," suggested Salem. "We can cover more mirrors that way."

"Yeah, and get twice as lost," Hilda pointed out cheerfully.

"No, I think Salem has a good idea," said Zelda. "Drell's tall enough to see over the mirrors. If one of us finds the right mirror, we can signal him and he can guide the rest of us to it."

"That's me," cracked Drell. "A pillar of the community, a compass in the wilderness, a beacon to the masses . . ."

Hilda grabbed his hand, pulling him forward again. "C'mon, beacon boy, let's start looking."

Sabrina watched them head down a path that she hadn't even recognized as a path. "Boy, these mirrors can be so confusing!" she complained.

Salem shook his head and sighed. "You have such a way with the obvious."

"Don't you two start bickering," Zelda warned. "We have enough friction between Hilda and Drell." She faced the nearest mirror, checking out her Elizabethan-dressed reflection. "This is quite elegant and much less uncomfortable than when I last wore one, but I don't know if it would qualify as 'cool.'"

One hour and endless outfits later, Sabrina, Zelda, and Salem were still looking. They'd seen their reflections in safari gear, Girl Scout uniforms, tutus, tuxedos, miniskirts, and Dr. Denton's long johns. They'd seen what they'd look like as firemen, lab technicians, garbage collectors, and high-fashion models. But they hadn't yet found anything that would clearly constitute "cool" to Libby.

Stepping in front of yet another mirror, Sabrina and Zelda gasped—they were wearing minuscule Brazilian-style thong bikinis. "Wowzers!" Salem yelped.

"Turn around this instant!" Zelda commanded the cat.

Salem slowly obeyed, only to blurt out, "Whoa!"

Sabrina whirled around to see what the mirror behind them revealed. She saw herself in a skintight black leather pantsuit with spike-heel pumps, spiked purple hair, and a safety pin through her nose. "That is so not me!"

"What, Sabrina—?" Zelda began.

Sabrina grabbed Zelda's shoulders, preventing her from turning around. "Never mind. Let's just get out of here before Drell finds this spot."

They passed a mirror that put them into cheerleader outfits, and Sabrina winced at this reminder of Libby. "We're never going to get out of here, are we?"

"We have to," Salem said. "I'm hungry."

"Look, there's Hilda and Drell," Zelda said, pointing.

Sabrina could see the other two witches' reflections far ahead, dressed in Renaissance garb. Sabrina was surprised to see how comfortable and natural the two looked dressed in such clothes, and then she remembered that they'd both lived through that era and *had* dressed in such clothes. But despite how comfortable they looked in the clothes, they did not look comfortable with each other. "Uh-oh," she told Zelda, "I think they've had a fight."

"I think you're right," Zelda said. "Pretend you don't notice."

The two groups met, the mirrors surrounding them reflecting them in sweat suits, funky floral housecoats, and bulbous clown costumes. Hilda and Drell stood with their arms crossed, pointedly not looking at each other.

"So," Zelda said brightly, "find anything?"

"Of course they didn't," said Salem. "They've been fighting."

"Salem!"

"What?" Salem asked innocently.

Drell was trembling with suppressed frustration. "If I had my powers I'd take that rotten kid and turn her into a match! One swipe against my shoe and 'poof!' Lights out!" He paused, nose twitching. *"AhCHOO!"*

"Oh, stop spitting and moaning, Drell," Hilda snapped. "Geez, grumble grumble grumble. You've been a broken record for the last hour. Gimme a break."

Drell glowered at her as if deciding which bone to start with.

"Oh, enough already," said Sabrina. "How are we going to get out of here?"

"Cool clothes," Salem pondered thoughtfully. "Cool clothes. So out of all the clothes ever made, Sabrina, what would Libby consider the coolest?"

"Whatever the coolest people are wearing," Sabrina answered. Then her eyes bugged. "That's it!" She started back the way she and Zelda had come. "Come on!"

"Where?" Zelda asked.

Sabrina led the group back to one particular mirror. "Stand in front of it," she ordered. Too hopeful to argue, they all stood in front of the mirror—and saw themselves dressed as cheerleaders. "The coolest people wear the coolest clothes," Sabrina explained. "Libby always says that cheerleaders are the coolest!"

"I don't know," ventured Salem. "She's never seen Drell in a pleated skirt and knee socks."

Sabrina tentatively reached out her hand and touched the mirror. The reflective surface was hard, but as she pushed, it suddenly gave way and her hand disappeared into it. "The doorway out?" she suggested.

"Let's go!" Zelda said.

An instant later they were back in the now-familiar topsy-turvy geometry of the mall. They didn't wait but a minute to gather their wits before clicking their way to the second test site.

This time they found themselves in front of a small store with a marble façade. It was the most ornate, elegant store design that Sabrina had ever seen. The outside positively glittered with polish and tasteful gilded accents. The store itself, however, seemed to consist of just a polished teak counter that faced the open etched-glass doors.

"Welcome to the Storage Store," greeted the handsome young man behind the rich wood counter.

"Harvey?" Sabrina gasped.

"Don't get excited, dear," cautioned Zelda.

"Remember that this is only Libby's version of Harvey, not the real thing."

On second look, Sabrina realized that she'd never seen her Harvey dressed so expensively, nor did she think she ever would. This Harvey was dressed to the nines in a custom-fitted Ralph Lauren lamé tuxedo. A diamond chip winked on the ring in his ear, and a massive solid gold Rolex peeped out from under a well-starched Chinese silk shirt. He positively oozed slickness and sophistication. "What can I show you fine folks today?" He smiled like a TV news anchorman.

Sabrina tried to pull her mind back to the business at hand. "Uh, we're supposed to solve a riddle here." She pressed the slip of paper with the poem on it into his immaculately manicured hand.

He read the poem out loud:

"Fancy wax and carmine dye,
In a storage box am I.
Standard gear for female mortal
Will provide an exit portal."

A look of mild confusion clouded his face and he handed the paper back to Sabrina. "Sorry," he said. "I don't think I can help you out on that one. This is about content, and we don't have much call for that here."

"What?"

Harvey waved his hand languidly at the tiny store. "We specialize in packaging, not contents. We sell fancy boxes, containers, and exotic wrapping. Our motto is, 'Who cares what's inside as long as the packaging is great?' It's sorta symbolic, you see. If something looks just like something better, then it's as good as having the real thing. Better, sometimes, because with a good enough package, you don't need *anything* inside."

"But how is this supposed to help us solve the riddle?"

"Beats me," the fake Harvey confessed, examining his reflection in a gilt-framed mirror. He slid his hands smoothly across his hair, even though not a strand was out of place. "That involves thinking, and I don't like the wrinkles that makes. We have a storeroom filled with stuff in the back, if you want to poke around. Maybe you'll find what you want there." He began inspecting his suit for lint.

As he spoke, a richly carved door appeared in the back wall and swung silently open.

"Haven't we been through this routine before?" yawned Salem.

"If you know the drill, why are you wasting time?" said Hilda, scooping the cat up and marching toward the door. The others followed in single file. Once again, as soon as the door closed behind them, it disappeared.

In sharp contrast to the tiny storefront they'd

entered through, the storeroom could have held four or five aircraft carriers and still had room to squeeze in an ordinary-sized mall, parking lot and all.

The cavernous space was not empty, though. Miles of steel shelving gridded the floor, towering upward into the dim mists obscuring the ceiling far overhead. Stairs and catwalks crisscrossed the shelving, providing access to all of the boxes stored in the room. An infinite variety of boxes. At least one, Sabrina imagined, of every possible kind of containerlike object.

Starting with the cheapest, there were paper bags of every kind of color, print, and pattern sorted into pigeonholes that were, in themselves, forms of storage. Cardboard boxes, from pill-sized to monstrous corrugated supercrates, lined shelves and sat atop walls built from their stacked brethren. Plastic containers sat mutely on bulwarks of wooden chests, endlessly varied by wood, finish, carving, and ornamentation.

Those were just the beginning, Sabrina realized. In keeping with the store's upscale pretensions, the majority of the containers in the room were rare, precious, or unique in materials, design, and manufacture. There was, in fact, every kind of thing she could imagine sticking something else into and many more that she'd never even dreamed of.

As the five of them stood mutely in shock at the daunting search ahead of them, the door to the front of the store reappeared and opened. Harvey darted in with a mailbox in his hands, quickly setting it down on a table near the door. He grinned apologetically, saying, "Sorry. Late arrival." An instant later, he was back out the door, and the door itself had vanished again.

"How in the Sam Hill are we supposed to find anything in here?" groused Salem loudly. "Especially when we don't even know what we're looking for?"

Zelda walked to the nearest shelf and lifted the lid of a box to peer inside. "I guess we'll just have to start looking," she said. Zelda and Sabrina walked to different shelves and started inspecting as well. Salem leaped up to the second tier of shelves and started pawing at the paper bags.

Drell watched the witches and the cat poke at containers with rapidly evaporating patience. His face darkened until he finally exploded. "The rest of you can waste time with this higgledy-piggledy poking around if you want. But if you want real results, do it my way!"

He stomped over to the nearest shelves and grabbed the uprights in meaty hands. With a mighty wrench, he toppled all the boxes off the shelves and onto the floor. Lids popped open, corners split, and some of the more fragile containers shivered to pieces. Drell glared at the mess for a moment and then announced, "Nothing in these." He moved on to the next shelf, toppling that in turn.

Sabrina recoiled before the giant witch's fury. *I don't suppose I can blame him,* she thought. *After all, he's been all-powerful so long that not having powers must be driving him crazy.*

Hilda was staring at Drell's increasing swath of destruction with irritation. "If you have a problem you need solved, call a woman," she sneered. "If you want to make a bigger problem out of it, call a man." Obviously, Drell's allure had recently diminished somewhat in her eyes.

A wave of depression threatened to drown Sabrina. Finding a way of retrieving Drell's lost powers from Libby seemed hopeless, even if they succeeded in solving this puzzle. Were they doomed to live in a universe of superficiality and status-consciousness? Looking at the mailbox, she thought of the Libby-ized Harvey out in the store. Sure, he was gorgeous in his fancy attire, but there didn't seem to be anyone home inside the glamorous exterior.

The homely mailbox reminded Sabrina of the real Harvey—shy, sometimes awkward, but with unexpected depths and insights. *Like his fascination with mailboxes,* she thought. *I'll bet he knows every mailbox in Westbridge.* The depression deepened into a feeling of hopelessness teetering on the abyss of despair. She walked over to the mailbox and lifted it in her hands. *I'm sorry I did this to you, Harvey.*

Something rattled inside the mailbox. Sabrina pried open the flap and peered inside. There *was* something inside. Tilting the mailbox with one hand, she rolled the object out into the palm of the other. It was a cylinder of teal anodized aluminum with the initials "LC" stamped on one side. A paper label on one end identified it as Pom-Pom Pink Lipstick. *Great!* Sabrina thought glumly. *Libby-brand lipstick by Special Delivery.*

The words of the poem suddenly came racing back to her. *What's lipstick except wax and red coloring? Isn't carmine a shade of red?* She started shouting excitedly, "I found it! Everybody, come here! I found it!"

Salem bounded down from the catwalk and hopped daintily over spilled boxes to come to Sabrina. Hilda and Zelda took less direct but equally careful paths back to their niece. Drell simply kicked his way through shattered containers, making his own path as he came.

Sabrina held up the lipstick for all to see. "I think I've found what we were supposed to find, but I don't know how it's supposed to get us out of here."

"Might as well try the simplest approach first," said Hilda, taking the lipstick tube from Sabrina's hands and yanking the top open.

Nothing happened.

"Is this what we were looking for?" said Sabrina. "Or is Libby cheating?"

Hilda shook her head. "I don't think the Rules Bearer would let her cheat, as much as she might want to."

"Then what do we do next?"

"Let's see," mused Zelda. "The lipstick fits the poem, so I'm sure that we've gotten that part right. The last line is, 'Will provide an exit portal,' so there must be a way to use it to get out."

"Right," scoffed Drell. "How is a glorified crayon supposed to help us get out of here?"

Hilda put her hands on her hips. "Drell, did you ever hear the expression, 'if you can't say anything nice, don't say anything at all'?"

"No, but if you hum a few bars, I'll fake it," Drell said with an irritating smirk.

"Grrr!" Hilda pursed her lips, her eyes narrow as she regarded her ex-boyfriend. "You know, I can't for the life of me figure out what I ever saw in you. You're rude, nasty, ill-tempered, tyrannical, and interested only in yourself."

Flexing his biceps, Drell beamed at her. "That's me—a perfect specimen of manhood."

"Wait a minute," Zelda interrupted. "Sabrina, do you remember what the Harvey outside said about symbolism?"

Sabrina sifted back through her memory. "I think he said something about the symbolic things being just as good as the real thing. That's a Libby thought if I ever heard one."

"But magic is symbolic, too," Zelda explained. "When we cast spells, we use symbolic things like feathers and herbs to make us think of certain properties, then we use our magic power to make those things real."

"So you put on the lipstick and kiss this place good-bye?" cracked Salem.

Zelda ignored the cat, walking instead to the nearest wall and using the lipstick to draw the outline of a door. She added a circle to represent the doorknob and then stepped back. "Would you do the honors, Sabrina?"

Sabrina looked doubtful, but reached out as if to grasp the red circle like a real knob. To her surprise, she felt cold roundness turn under her hand. There was a sound of cracking plaster, and the rectangle of the door swung open to reveal the interior of the mall.

☆

Chapter 14

☆

The last "clicka" transported Sabrina and her companions to a large, comfortable room with stylish, modern furnishings—lots of furnishings, in fact. A variety of couches, a dozen plush chairs, and several coffee tables were artfully arranged across a large Persian carpet. Potted plants and flower arrangements tastefully accented the scene. Sabrina thought the place looked like a high-class waiting room.

Occupying one corner was a polished wooden desk behind which sat a familiar face. "Cassandra!" Drell boomed, genuinely pleased to see her.

Cassandra, a lovely witch who, along with Drell and Skippy, comprised the Witches' Council, stood up from her chair. When Sabrina had last seen her, she'd been wearing a long, black,

Gothic-style dress and had looked quite witchy and exotic. Now she sported a slick business suit and her luxurious blond hair was pulled back and secured in a tight bun. "Drell," she said in a flat, official tone. "Ms. Chessler has been expecting you."

"Ms. Chessler?" Zelda asked in surprise.

Cassandra regarded them with amusement. "Of course. You *are* in her office. If you'll excuse me, I'll have you announced." She vanished in a puff of smoke.

Drell watched her go with a look of pain. "Cassandra—an executive secretary? How cold can you get?"

"Drell, didn't you hear what she said?" Sabrina whispered, panicked. "This is Libby's office! I thought we had to face another challenge and win before we got to see her!"

Zelda pulled a piece of paper from her pocket. It was one of the airplanes that contained Libby's challenge hints. She unfolded it and read, "'Prepare for the Ultimate Challenge.' That's all it said."

"I guess trying to take power away from Libby qualifies," Sabrina had to admit.

"Uh, I may be bringing this up a little late in the game," Hilda ventured, "but now that we're about to actually see Libby, what exactly are we going to do?"

Everybody looked stunned except Drell, who vehemently whispered, *"We're* not going to do anything. *I'm* going to sneeze into that meddle-some mortal's face and get my powers back!"

"Easy, Drell," Zelda cautioned. "The minute Libby sees you, she'll turn you into a toad. We've got to think of a way to distract her."

Salem leaped up on Cassandra's empty desk. "Whatever we do, we'd better do it fast. We may not have much time."

"I've got it," Sabrina said suddenly. "I've got a plan." She crouched down so that she faced Salem eye-to-eye. "And it all depends on you."

Salem's whiskers drooped. "That's right, leave the dirty work to the cat."

"Just listen," Sabrina said. "This is what we have to do . . ."

Libby sat on her throne, basking in the right-ness of things. It was only right that she was now, for all intents and purposes, a goddess. It was only right that she'd taken her place as leader of the Other Realm, disbanding the ridiculous Witches' Council and molding the realm to fit her whim. And it was only right that she now eliminate the last unpleasant aspect of her for-mer life—Sabrina Spellman.

Libby knew that Sabrina had regained her own powers, but obviously the little freak was no match for her, not now. Yes, Sabrina and her glee club had succeeded in passing the first two of Libby's challenges, but the last one wasn't going to be so easy. Libby hadn't figured out how to handle all the aspects of Drell's powers yet—she had the strength and the talent but not the centuries of magical lore. No matter, she was a quick learner. Look what she'd already accomplished.

She surveyed her throne room with satisfaction. Libby adored this room. She'd used her magic to create the most perfect place in the world: a gallery devoted exclusively to her. The huge rectangular chamber qualified as a cavern more than a room, and every inch of wall space had been covered with accolades to her greatness. Framed blowup photos of her on all the world's major magazine covers adorned the west wall. Newspaper clippings praising her covered the east wall. Statues of her, including a sparkling fountain featuring her bronze form gracefully posed in the center of a shower of crystalline water, occupied various pedestals scattered at intervals across the vast floor, each piece of art bathed it its own witch-light illumination.

A long red carpet led up to her throne. At the opposite end of it, a set of great double doors slowly opened. Sabrina, looking small and appropriately insignificant, entered, followed by her busybody aunts and, last of all, Libby's unintentional benefactor, Drell. Libby sprang to her feet, jabbing her index finger in the air, freezing Drell in his tracks.

"Well," Libby said cheerfully as she relaxed

back into her throne, "that takes care of that. A witch in deep freeze is a witch who can't sneeze, right?" She flicked her finger twice, and Sabrina's aunts became statuary as well. Libby's heart swelled with satisfaction as she saw Sabrina's face fall. "Oh, please," she said. "It's not like I didn't know what you're up to. Don't worry, I'll put them in a garden or something, okay?"

To Libby's surprise, Sabrina bowed her head in submission. "All right, Libby. You win."

"I do?" squeaked Libby. "I mean, of course I do!"

Sabrina twitched her fingers slightly and a stunningly ornamented box appeared in her outstretched hands. Made of beaten gold and encrusted with gems and rare cloisonné, its weight made her struggle to hold it in front of her. "As a token of my submission, please allow me to present you with this small coronation gift."

"Gift accepted," Libby said smugly. But as Sabrina stepped forward, Libby's raised finger stopped her in her tracks. "You're very clever, I'm sure," she said. "But I'm smarter. You stay right there. I'll fetch the gift."

A wave of her hand and the box floated out of Sabrina's immobile hands, down the long red carpet and up the steps to the throne. Libby's eyes widened in greed as she saw the richness of the box and the overabundance of filigree and exquisite tooling. "Your taste is improving, Sabrina. Perhaps there's hope for you yet," she gloated as the box settled on her lap.

As soon as the box stopped moving, the top sprang open. Inside the box, a black Burmese cat grinned up at her. "If the box looks . . . *sniff* . . . good enough," he said, sniffling, "it doesn't matter what's inside, right?" Then he sneezed directly into Libby's face.

Chapter 15

A shimmer ran through reality as Libby's stolen powers fled her body. All around her the mall soundlessly shivered into a billion transparent fragments and twinkled out of existence. A boundless blue sky flecked with fluffy cumulus clouds faded into place as the mall vanished. Leaves and vines snaked through the air like a time-lapse movie to form carpeted pathways and furnishings that floated in midair. Slowly and majestically, a giant apple on a marble pedestal rose like a green sun. Within seconds, the Other Realm was restored to the way it had been before Libby changed it.

With her power now gone, all the effects of Libby's magic disappeared as well. The Spellman aunts snapped into motion as their magical paralysis was removed. Zelda pointed at Libby, who suddenly found herself in a small, transparent room floating within the blue space. Frustrated and furious, Libby's mouth moved but no sound escaped the room.

Hilda levitated the gold box containing the cat to a place on the restored Council table, allowing the feline to jump out and stretch. "That was fun," he said. "It's good to be omnipotent again." He looked up at Hilda. "Uh . . . mind changing me back to my own body?"

"Not so fast," said Sabrina, approaching the table with "Drell" by her side. "We have a few details to iron out first."

"You dare to set conditions on me? Overlord of the Universe? Head of the Witches' Council? Now that I have my powers back, I'll—"

"Do nothing at all," finished Zelda, coming up to loom over the cat. "You know very well that, without being able to point, you can't use your powers. You have to listen to us."

"Yeah," added Hilda. "It was Sabrina's idea to switch bodies between you and Salem so you could sneak up on Libby and get your powers back. We can't let you do terrible things to her after all her hard work."

"I wasn't planning on doing anything to her," replied Drell almost sincerely. "It's Libby I was going to disassemble, along with turning a certain cat into a chafing dish."

"I can't let you hurt any of my friends," said

Sabrina. "If you won't promise to leave them alone, you can stay a cat for eternity."

"I'll vote for that," rumbled Salem, flexing Drell's arms and admiring the muscles. "I could get comfortable wearing this body."

"You keep out of this," snapped Hilda. "We haven't forgotten all the trouble you've caused us."

Drell tried to stand on his cat hind legs and loom over the witches like he normally did, but succeeded only in falling facedown on the table. He recovered and shook with repressed fury. "I have to destroy Libby. She knows too much to be allowed to leave."

"Wrong!" said Zelda. She waved at Libby in the transparent box, and the cheerleader suddenly slumped gently to the floor and began to snore. "We put her into a separate room so that she wouldn't regain your powers if you sneezed again, but we're not going to let you harm her. I've wiped her memory of the whole affair, so that when she wakes up she'll remember nothing. She isn't a threat to any of us anymore."

Drell twitched his tail in annoyance but finally relented. "Oh, all right," he said grumpily. "But Salem is going to be a buffet tray for my Sunday brunches."

"You don't do anything to anybody," Sabrina threatened, "or it's fleas forever."

"Yes, yes. Whatever you say. Now change me back."

"Just a minute," said Zelda. She addressed the empty air. "Oh, Rules Bearer." In a flash, the petite enforcer of the rules appeared. Zelda pointed at the cat. "Now say it again."

"What, you don't trust my word?"

"Rule 1102: All Promises Made In The Presence Of The Rules Bearer Shall Be Binding Upon All Parties Forever."

"It's a sad state of affairs when witches don't trust their own leader."

"Let's just say that your reputation precedes you, Drell," Zelda observed dryly. "Now, promise."

Drell fidgeted, then rapidly said, "IDrell promisenottoharmLibbyChesslerorSalemthecat foranythingthey'vedoneupuntilnow."

"Duly witnessed," said the Rules Bearer. "Well, gotta go. Anybody seen where Skippy wound up?" Receiving no answer, she disappeared in a cloud of lavender-scented smoke.

Zelda waved her hands over the cat body. "Drell and Salem are back where they belong," she intoned. There was a flash of light and then the cat jumped up into Sabrina's arms.

"It's been great fun, but it's time to go," said Salem.

Drell flexed his massive bulk, as if shrugging into an old, familiar outfit. "Wisdom comes with age, cat," purred the giant. "Pray you live long enough to develop some. You're clear for now, but I'm gonna be waiting for you when you make that next wrong step." He fixed his flat gaze on the rest of the Spellmans. "Now get Sleeping Beauty out of here before I charge you all with loitering."

Zelda and Sabrina levitated Libby's cube and raced for the linen closet.

A flash of light and a peal of thunder later, three witches and a cat stepped out into the second-floor hallway of the Spellman house. Libby, still asleep, floated behind them. With an economical gesture, Zelda made the unconscious girl vanish. "That takes care of her," she said tiredly. "Although she's going to wonder why she fell asleep in the back of the school auditorium." She looked at her sister and her niece. "I think it's time to collapse on the couch with a big bowl of popcorn. Care to join me?"

"Count me in," chirped Hilda, following her sister down the stairs. Her voice floated back up to Sabrina as she descended. "You know, for a while there Drell was a real pain in the you-know-where, but now that he's got his powers back, he's kind of cute again."

"I don't know what you see in that man," Zelda said.

"You just don't understand the attraction of a real challenge. . . ."

As her aunts' voices faded, Sabrina yawned and turned to face Salem. "I just don't understand how you could even think about making a deal with Libby."

"Let's just say I have a fatal weakness when it comes to world domination," Salem said. "Besides, Libby's not such a bad person, if you like style over substance."

"So I guess that means that if I glue on premium labels, we can feed you the discount cat food from now on?"

As Sabrina stumbled tiredly into her bedroom, Salem put his head down on his paws. "It's always the cat that gets the raw end of the deal."

About the Authors

DAVID CODY WEISS and BOBBI JG WEISS are writing partners. They're also married. They have lots of cats and cactus plants, and they like to keep toys in the living room. Day after day they slog away at their computers, wracking their brains to write up fanciful and often absurd stories that they then sell to publishers for money. They have written a whole lot of stuff, among them novels (two for the *Are You Afraid of the Dark?* series, two Starfleet Academy novels, *Breakaway* and *Lifeline,* and *The Secret World of Alex Mack: Close Encounters);* novel adaptations *(Jingle All the Way; Sabrina, the Teenage Witch);* comic books *(Pinky and the Brain, Animaniacs);* trading cards *(Batman and Robin, Star Trek Universe, James Bond Connoisseur Collection);* and other weird stuff like clothing tag blurbs, office catalog copy, and little squeezy books for kids who can't read yet so they just look at the pictures and squeeze the squeezy toy.

Bobbi and David hope to be filthy rich one day because laughing all the way to the bank sounds like fun.